EXCLUSION ZONE

PETER J ALDIN

Cover art:

Alexandre Rito

Professional editing/proofing:

BB Burdock and Sheena Billett

To Mark and to Dave.
You both know which Mark and Dave I mean.
And you know why I'm grateful.

July, 3001, Old Earth Calendar

Chapter 1: Dog Team

"Our settled worlds have spent a century emerging from the Second Dark Age. But we've been slow to recapture the halcyon days of interstellar exploration. And we continue to fall short of the technological superiority of the 22nd century.

Some of this 'tech-lag' is planned by our government(s), a form of caution and self-distinction. After all, the Confederation's governing belief is that the best route forward means embracing the unity of past civilizations while avoiding their errors.

One of these pathways to unity is through language.

Since the mid-30th century, the first member-worlds of the Democratic Confederation of Human Colonies encouraged the revival of three standardized 22nd century languages: English, Spanish and Mandarin. The rationale behind this was to fuel reunification and progress, to foster commonality, and to remove cultural barriers.

By the dawn of the 31st century, the three

standardized languages have become known in slang as Conglish, Espancon and Condarin."

Iverson, Cohan & Kalili, *The Reunification of Human Civilization - a History of Recovery after the Second Dark Age*, Dogstar Press, 2998, page 193

THE ASSAULT SKIFF WAS A PREDATOR, its prey a cargo runner.

The freighter floated adrift with its thrusters slagged and its shield generators powered down while the skiff sped toward it.

In contrast to the target vehicle's boxy shape, the assault skiff was roughly torpedo-shaped, an armored tube ornamented with acceleration thrusters and braking jets. To maintain the sleek, efficient design, no stubby airlocks poked from its sides. Rather, the designers had placed the boarding lock up front, and the pilot station in back, servicing the pilot with multiple outboard cameras and a continuous external feed from its distant launch vehicle for reference.

Built for swift crossings from launch vehicle to target vehicle, the skiff had *not* been built for comfort. Peacekeeper Marine Private Denise Westermann was experiencing this fact yet again. Acceleration and vector changes bounced her around in her crash rack. The bigger versions she'd ridden in other star systems had been newer models, with top-quality inertial dampeners.

They'd been smooth; this old thing was rougher than a fairground ride.

She fidgeted and swore. A little rough treatment she could live with. No one with a weak stomach made it through BASIC. But the dumbass shippy who'd harnessed her up had hurried the task, leaving Westermann to suffer the consequences. Her boarding team had been issued with the latest-model combat e-suits, lighter-armored and therefore more flexible than the predecessor version she was used to. Up till now, Westermann had been grateful for the upgrade. They'd been comfortable enough during drills. Right now, because of that shippy's shitty harnessing job, the lighter suit-material had allowed a couch strap to ride up into the crease where her thigh met her groin.

Across from her in the cramped cabin, Private Jeng watched on as she struggled to hook a gloved thumb under the tight belt strap. Visible through his helmet visor, the man's face radiated concern. She'd decided Jeng was a nice guy the moment he'd arrived in the Zuchola Exclusion Zone two weeks back. Polite, ready to help, quick to laugh at her jokes, happy to share the mountain of info floating around that gigantic brain of his. But Jeng was maybe *too* nice for a dog team. Definitely too nice to be hanging out with the guys who made up half of *this* team.

Only one way to find out if he's built for this, she thought, trying to smile back at Jeng and take her mind off the damn thigh strap. *Ya do the thing. Ya do the job. Ya find out if you're fit for it.*

The four junior members of the team had been racked

in along the skiff's side bulkheads. A sudden, hard deceleration threw Westermann to her left, dislodging her grip on the harness. From two previous years of jobs like this in other star systems, she knew the jolt was a good sign. They were almost at target. She checked her helmet HUD which blinked and flashed with the icons, numbers, and acronyms of constantly updating data streams. The figure on the RTT counter confirmed it. *Range-to-target* was now a mere thirty-eight klicks.

Giving up on the strap, she caught Jeng's eye again.

Goddamn, he looks nervous.

Today would be his first hard-contact mission.

Hell, she thought. *In this system at least, it's* my *first hard-contact too. Been a while.*

She pointed down at the offending strap. "Ya think those Navy chubs have a competition? See who can rack us in the uncomfortablest?"

Via her helmet speaker, his voice was clear, if shaky. "I think it's 'least comfortably.'"

"What?"

"I think the correct English is 'least comfortably.'"

She snorted. "The Maoan who grew up speaking Mandarin is gonna tell me how to speak English?"

Her attempt at distracting them both failed when the thigh strap slipped a millimeter higher, pressed a millimeter tighter. If it got much worse, she'd be pissing in her suit. Westermann hated pissing in her suit. "*Goddamn* this hacking thing!"

A different voice sounded in her headset, this one coarse and steady and brimming with self-importance. "Want some help there, powderpuff?"

She cringed; couldn't help it; shook it off as quick as she could. But *whenever* Badillo spoke to her directly, she cringed. Whenever he came into physical contact with her, she cringed. There'd been a *lot* of cringing since she'd been posted here. The mustache-lipped moron was a creep—*The* Creep, in her mind. Always hitting on the ladies, always hitting on *her* despite six months of telling him he was as attractive as a freshly laid turd.

When he offered again, Westermann chose not to reply. Replying would only encourage him.

You can choose your friends, went the Peacekeeper Corps saying, *but we choose your teammates.* And they'd chosen her some bad ones over the first two years of her career.

Badillo was harnessed in beside her where it was easy to avoid eye contact. But as the skiff shuddered and jolted to starboard, his suit leaned hard into hers, and his gloved hand landed on her thigh, then edged toward the offending harness strap.

She batted the offending hand away and said, "Hack you."

Badillo chuckled, wiggling around in his harness, jostling her again.

The guy to Jeng's left caught her eye as she made another attempt at adjusting the strap. "Crotch itch?"

"And hack you too, Badawi," she replied.

Badillo chuckled again, kicking one boot against Badawi's. "Blondie here's a feisty one, that's for shaz."

"Feisty, feisty, feisty," Badawi crooned in agreement. "Feisty little powderpuff."

Jeng watched the exchange with wary eyes and an

5

open mouth, as if ready to intervene but unsure how to. And in the back of the cabin, jammed into a crash rack bolted to the front of the pilot station and facing along the short cabin, Sergeant DeLuca shook his head behind his visor, an exasperated parent tired of scolding his children.

Children, she thought with another grimace. *I'm surrounded by 'em.*

Badillo. Corporal. The Creep. Always quick to check the fittings on a woman's environment suit, always brushing up against Westermann in passageways.

Badawi. The Killjoy. The sour-faced tech-jacker and suspiciously lucky poker player.

Jeng. The Noo Guy. The polite Maoan, the "late bloomer" who'd joined the PKs as a second career after growing bored with flying police skimmers on Mao.

And Child Number Four, Westermann thought. *Little ol' me. About to end yet another sucky six-month rotation. A sucky, boring six-month deployment to the ass-end of Confederation space. Where nothing important ever happens until the exact hackin' moment your leave rolls round and just for once you wanna to get home in time for your dad's hackin' birthday.*

She slid a palm up across the torso of her suit until it pressed against the baby shenty's skull clipped over her sternum, over her heart. Roughly the size of her ungloved thumb, she'd found the thing in their ranch's back paddock twelve years ago, the remains of a lamb who'd succumbed to the unseasonably hot weather the previous birthing season. Her mother had scolded her for bringing it into the house and binned it—and the next day her father had secretly retrieved it from the trash, varnished it, and gifted it back to her.

Shenty skulls had a beak at one end, a kind of short horn useful for digging up roots when grasses were scarce or dry. Her dad could have filed this beak when he'd polished it; instead he'd left that tiny aspect of danger, something that could hurt her if she wore it and fell on it, something she'd have to be careful with. Other PKs always assumed Westermann hung the skull on her suit to look more bad-ass. And she let them think that. The real reason was very different...

In her two years as a Peacekeeper, Westermann had never served on-planet. She'd always been posted aboard Confederation Navy vessels or stations that were scattered throughout Confederation space. Those postings lasted four to ten months at a time—and there'd been times when it became real easy to believe she'd never walked in the open air, never had grass tickling the soles of her feet, never been a rancher's daughter in a temperate region of an agricultural planet at all. All those things could easily feel like imagination, someone else's life. The skull reassured her that Centauri her homeworld was real, that her growing up years actually happened, and that her father was out there somewhere wishing her well and ever proud of her.

Thanks, Dad, she thought as she pinched it between thumb and forefinger. *Sometimes wonder what the hell I was thinking joining up ...*

Another sharp jerk of deceleration. The RTT counter read *1.21km.* She gave the shenty skull a gentle squeeze before clenching her fists in her lap, resisting the urge to tease at the irritating thigh strap in case it drew Badillo and Badawi's attention again. Time to focus. Time to make ready. Get her game face on. Do the job right, do it quick. Get out of here in time to make the supply shuttle back to Centauri and home.

As if reading her thoughts, Badillo asked her, "Whatcha got planned for your downtime, Westie? Or should I say *who ya got planned*?"

Turning her faceplate to his, she said, "I'm meeting your wife for a beer. Updating her on all your failed attempts at cheating on her."

Mock-laughing, he broke eye contact and leaned his head back in his rack.

"Mind on the job, Marines," barked DeLuca, finally intervening.

"Always, Sarge," she replied. A huffing sound in the speakers was Badillo's only acknowledgment of the order.

A bump and swing of orientation in the skiff, the pilot lining up their airlock with the target vessel's.

Across from her, Jeng's gloved hands had grabbed the harness over his chest, his thumbs tapping out a fast rhythm. His nerves, she figured, were not only under-standable, they were probably appropriate ...

The blockade at Zuchola had been in existence for thirty years. While a handful of sightseers had dropped by in the last decade or so, no one had ever actually tried to run it. And no one *had* a ship capable of getting past the skiff's launch ship, the compact interdictor *Artemis*. Also, Westermann thought, this star system had only one leap-point in and out. Easy to monitor, easy to block. Everyone these days knew that just coming out here bought you a one-way ticket to a short-term jail sentence. Everyone, apparently, except for the hackheads in the cargo runner they were about to board.

But if things ever *did* hit the fan around here, if some dumbass made it through and landed on Zuchola, and they somehow released another goddamned pandemic—

This is why your Dad's proud of you, she told herself. *Because as boring and un-hacking-comfortable as this is, it's hackdamn important.*

A wink and a thumbs-up at Jeng. *You'll be fine,* she mouthed at him. He returned the gesture.

"So sweet," mocked Badawi.

"Ship-strike in five counts," announced the pilot. Moments later, the floor shuddered and the cabin rocked as the skiff made its controlled collision with the freighter. "Clamps are set!"

Instantly, DeLuca added, "On me!" and smacked the fast release on his harness.

Once he'd stomped past them, his four subordinates hit their releases in unison, put their magboots to the floor and rose, reaching for rifles from the overheads. As she joined DeLuca at the skiff's forward airlock ahead of the other three Peacekeepers, Westermann jiggled her leg to force blood back into the thigh muscle, grimacing against a spike of pins and needles. DeLuca stepped into the lock —a box three meters deep, three wide, two high. Westermann came in beside him. Being in that box brought her a brief wave of claustrophobia as the other three PKs squeezed in at her back and the inner hatch sealed behind them. The feeling was mild, familiar, and easy to shake off. It was also a reminder she had a date with a big, wide open sky on her father's farm on Centauri …

All the things I just love about the job, she thought.

When DeLuca took a knee, she copied him, allowing the rear group clearance to fire over their heads when the outer hatch opened, if that was necessary.

"Braced," DeLuca informed the pilot.

A few last-minute knocks and jolts as the small vessel aligned with the cargo runner's lock and that ship's "up-down" orientation. Beyond the outer hatch, forcer-cables and smart-wire feelers battled the freighter's stubborn airlock seal until a terse "Got it!" from the pilot announced a connection was made.

A tiny image appeared in a corner of Westermann's HUD, vision from the freighter airlock's interior via one of the smart-wires. The interior door of the airlock had opened, revealing a slice of the passage beyond it, plus three cargo crewers down on their knees with their hands clasped on top of their heads.

Please let that be all of them, she thought.

Beside her, DeLuca pinged the interdictor hanging out in space two hundred klicks away. "You seein' this, *Artemis*?"

"Crystal," the *Artemis*'s Executive Officer replied, the sneer noticeable in her voice. She sniffed. "I see three scavvers making ready for their own arrests. Proceed with caution, dog team. Might be bogeys in the hallway."

"Yes, sir," DeLuca said, then paused his ship-comms with an angry stab at his arm panel. "Hackdamned shippy tellin' me my job."

"Shall we *do* our job, Sarge?" Westermann asked. The adrenaline in her system—the antsiness she felt—it had more to do with wanting to get this done and catch the transport home than it did about the people on the other side of this hatch.

DeLuca reached for the hatch control. "Three, two ..."

He nudged it and slapped that hand back onto his rifle. Westermann's fingers tightened on hers as the hatch snapped sideways into the hull. She was looking into the freighter's airlock for real now, seeing the same scene overlayed in miniature on her HUD: the four meters of open compartment with the three crewers kneeling in the passage beyond it. Two were men—their skin gray from lack of sunshine, their hair messy and greasy—the other an older woman—hair cleaner and tidier, but skin as gray as the males.

Westermann and DeLuca rose to march across the boarding seal.

"Keep ya hands there!" DeLuca yelled through his suit's external speaker.

Moving in sync with him, Westermann barked her own order at the crewers. "Do *not* move until we tell you!"

She stopped inside the airlock's interior doorway, keeping to the right, DeLuca the left, while the unhappy cargo crewers cowered just beyond it. She glanced back. Jeng had come to the middle of the airlock and taken a knee. Badillo and Badawi remained in the skiff's lock, just in case things went to crap.

"Okay, folks," she told the crewers. "Get down on your asses and shuffle back to the bulkhead." Blank looks. "I said—"

The woman—kneeling between the two men—raised her chin. "Neet scheetsen! Neet, arssubleef."

11

Westermann groaned. DeLuca cursed.

"That's Pollux-Dutch," Jeng said from behind them.

"That a fact?" DeLuca snapped without taking his focus from the detainees. "And do ya speak it, noog?"

"Uh … no."

"Then shut up with the trivia." He glanced at Westermann. "You?"

She'd come across the fringe language during other dog team missions a few times—and in bars. Shrugging, she replied, "Couple phrases is all."

The woman risked lowering a hand to tug at a chain around her neck. A curve-edged cross appeared from beneath her t-shirt, a cross engraved with a series of arcane runes. "Pelgrima. Pelgrima."

Westermann squinted at the runes then snorted. Those symbols—and that word—she recognized. "If you were pilgrims, there'd be more of you. That's a Family of Fire cross. Family of Fire members only travel in groups of twelve."

"Good point," DeLuca muttered. "Those hackers love their sacred number."

The woman gave up on the cross, letting it dangle as she returned the hand to her head. "Lost, lost, lost," she tried next.

Behind them, Badillo burst out laughing at the ploy.

"You ain't lost," DeLuca sneered at her. "No one can get lost enough to end up here."

"On your butts and move back," Westermann told them.

None showed any sign of understanding. The woman rattled off more rapid-fire gibberish that Westermann's mind couldn't pattern into sentences: "Scheetsen neet arssubleef vye zie allemaal ouders vye hebben kinderen om naar huis te qhayn."

"Pretty sure they don't want you to shoot," Jeng said.

"Very helpful," DeLuca grumbled. He told the pilot, "Run the translator prog in our HUDs."

"Copy."

Westermann groaned. There was enough distracting crap already flitting across the inside of her helmet. She really didn't want a text translation too. "Make mine audio-only."

Badawi laughed once. "Westie can't read. Didn't have school books back on the farm."

"Read this." She took one hand from her rifle long enough to give him the finger without looking back.

A few seconds later, her helmet speaker chirped with the prog coming online, and the pilot said, "Active," to confirm it.

Westermann waved her rifle toward the wall behind the detainees. "Back there. Get back."

Finally picking up her meaning, they shuffled back on their knees, making room.

"Goddamned lub-head Luxans," DeLuca muttered. "Shouldn't fly if they can't speak Conglish. *We* had to learn it ..." He gave Westermann a nod that meant, *You go in first.*

"Too kind," she muttered. She and the sergeant still stood within the airlock. First, she poked her rifle out into the passage and angled it toward the stern. The weapon's tiny camera fed her HUD the image of a clear corridor ending in a closed door five meters back. "Clear."

She withdrew the weapon, allowing DeLuca to do the same but check the way toward the bow.

"Clear," he reported.

The airlock decking shook a little as the rest of the team came out of the skiff and stacked up behind Westermann. Cargo runners like this, she knew, had passages along the port and starboard sides with compartments along the center. None of those compartments opened into both passageways, allowing the two men to clear them without fear of potential hostiles circling around and coming up behind them. Aft there'd be a broad empty decking in front of a passenger elevator, with the drive-and-systems maintenance compartment behind that lift. Depending on what lay in the large cargo holds above and below this central deck, clearing the ship should be pretty straightforward.

DeLuca gestured left with two fingers. Badillo bumped past Westermann, entered the passage and turned aft. Jeng followed at his heels, and she patted the noog's suit in reassurance as he passed. The sergeant entered the passage headed forwards with Badawi at his shoulder, planning to clear the cockpit before circling around the deck in the opposite direction to check the far side of the vessel.

This left Westermann alone with her trio of prisoners.

"Prisoners, detainees. They're the official words for you three." She stared them down while the suit's external speaker conveyed her words. "I prefer *scavvers*. Question is, what were you planning to scav, and what were you planning on doing with it?"

The corridor was tight, less than two meters wide. The

paneling looked solid, but any of these bulkheads could be screening secret compartments. Since this ship had working arti-grav, her boots were no longer magnetized, so she stamped one on the deck.

"Got a hidey-hole under there? Huh?"

"Vye zie qhayn smokkolors," one of the men jabbered. He had a thin mustache, a lot like Badillo's. He was also short and skinny and had a flat nose. Like Badillo. She took an instant dislike to him.

An English translation sounded softly in her suit speaker: *We're not smugglers.*

"Riiight," she said. "But you *are* scavengers, yeah?"

"Vye waren verdwaald," he replied, having to swallow to continue. "Eena shnook hot onz StarNav."

The translation prog said: *We got lost. Our StarNav had a glitch.*

Westermann snorted a laugh, prompting the guy to ramp up his insistence.

"Vye zie eerlyker zokenmansen!"

We are honest businesspeople.

Still grinning, Westermann held up a hand, silencing him. She indicated the other male, another skinny individual who had a charming and well-shaven face underneath the sweat and dirt. She told him, "Now, you try."

He swallowed, glanced at the others, then pleaded, "Arssubleef. Vye zie allemaal ouders. Vye hebben kinderen om naar huis te qhayn."

Please. We're all parents. We have children to go home to.

She raised her hand for silence again. They stared up at her with wide eyes, biting their lower lips.

"You're Family of Fire pilgrims. You're lost. You're

15

business people." The grin faded, as did her momentary amusement. These mutts were criminals. And they were delaying her preparations for shore leave. "You all need to listen to me, very carefully. I have heard this shit before. Thirty times before. In ten other languages. I really wanna get off this tub asap. And one of you definitely speaks English. Or Spanish. The Sarge was right about that: no way can you fly around the DCHC without speaking one of 'em, at least a little. So, shall we get on with this?"

She leaned in, rattled her rifle and pronounced her next words precisely.

"Who. Speaks. English."

"Farrdomme dits," mumbled the woman, then admitted, "I speak ... bit."

"Bit?" Westermann straightened. "Well, all right. A bit's better than nothing. Listen up. The others are completing their preliminary sweep. Pre-lim-in ..." The woman's eyes had narrowed in confusion. Westermann sighed. "They look quick around your ship."

The woman shrugged at that. "They look, see nothings. Just *our* things. We not ... smokkolors. We go at Bona Vista Station, but da StarNav hacky bad and it screw out."

"Screw *up*," Westermann corrected, then wondered why she'd bothered. "Just listen, lady. When they're done with the preliminary sweep, two of us Peacekeepers will take two of you back to *Artemis* for questioning. A Navy interrogator will try and find out what you wanted to steal from Zuchola. Why you idiots thought it was worth risking some new supervirus getting off of that hellhole."

"What is *arr-teem* ...?"

"*Artemis* is our interdictor. You know 'interdictor'?"

The woman wrinkled her face. "Is big ship for catch smokkelars, but we no smokkelars."

"Yeah. You said." She broke eye contact with the woman and focused on her comms. "Hey, team, you hearing this?"

"Most of it," said Badawi from somewhere forwards.

"It's hilarious," said Badillo back in the stern.

"And the funniest thing is how bad you are at scaring them," Badawi added.

"Hack you," she replied. "And are *you* actually accomplishing anything, killjoy? What have you found?"

"No bogeys, no contraband," DeLuca replied, interrupting. He sounded disappointed.

Jeng, in the stern with Badillo, said, "Looks like someone was refitting the leapdrive with spare parts before we arrived."

Westermann studied the crew's hands. The man with the mustache had carbon dust in the flesh between his fingers. "That woulda been Badillo's mustache-buddy here."

"Mustache ...?"

Jeng kept talking, his tone enthusiastic. "Fat chance of getting their drive running in less than an hour. Even their thrusters would take longer than that. *Artemis*'s ion strikes were surgical. Really great work. There's evidence of a small electrical fire back here, but nothing life threatening."

"I'm sure the Captain and XO will love hearing your review," DeLuca told him over comms.

A half minute's silence, then Westermann had to say, "Hurry it up, boys, will ya? Ship's not all that big. And I'd like to take my helmet—"

"On your right, Private," replied DeLuca.

She turned that way. Sure enough, the sergeant was headed back toward her.

He had *his* helmet off and swinging from one fist, and he'd secured his rifle to his suit's chestplate. His other hand carried a small plastic baggy bulging at the bottom. He waggled it at her, then tucked it inside a suit pouch. "Demon-frost. All I've found so far, but already enough to make their troubles worse. You *can* take ya bowl off now, Westie, if ya want. But you'll regret it, trust me."

"Why?"

He wrinkled his nose and waved a hand in the air.

"Oh." She'd experienced the "lived-in" odors of deep space vessels on many occasions, inspecting crappy old ships like this one with poor filtration and messy occupants.

"Take it off anyway. Suit samplers say zero pathogens. Cockpit panels say hull integrity's fine. *You*," DeLuca directed at the Polluxan with the lip hair. "Up. *Get up!* Right. Hands like this."

He tossed his helmet into the airlock out of the way, then applied wristcuffs to the guy, letting him keep his hands in front.

Westermann let her rifle hang from its strap. She got her helmet off and tossed it near DeLuca's, then sampled the passageway air. "Oh, *God*. What *is* that?"

Since her suit mic was in the collar, the other three heard her clear enough wherever they were placed around the freighter. Badillo and Badawi laughed from the comms speaker set in the other side of her collar.

Jeng replied, "Hygiene station looked pretty unpleasant as we passed it."

She took a deeper breath, regretting it as DeLuca had promised.

"God *damn* it."

She thought about replacing the helmet—but the things were more hindrance than help when a Marine wasn't under threat. And she was sick of looking at things through the HUD overlay. So, she left it off and concentrated on breathing through her mouth.

DeLuca grasped the shoulder of the man he'd cuffed. "I'll stick this one in the skiff for now, hook him up for early *intair*."

"What is intair?" asked the woman, still down on her knees with the other man.

"Interrogation," Westermann replied distractedly. "Appreciate you starting early, Sarge. Sooner, we're done …"

"Sooner you keep your date with an outbound transport. Sure, Westie. Everything I do is for your convenience." He had a rare, good-humored twinkle in his eye as he said it.

She checked the timestamp on her suit's wrist panels. The outbound transport had departed the research orbital above Zuchola more than an hour ago. That meant it would dock with *Artemis* in around seven hours.

Seven hours, she thought with a grimace. Ship searches could take a *lot* longer than that.

DeLuca spoke into his comms again. "Everyone ditch

your bowls. No reason me and Westie should have the stink all to ourself. Keep 'specting the back o' the boat, Badillo. Same with the cockpit, Badawi. Noog, get up here and help Westie with these detainees."

"Yes, Sarge."

While DeLuca covered her, Westermann deftly and swiftly searched the pair, making them stand in turn, patting them down, making them kneel again. Jeng arrived as she finished.

She asked DeLuca, "You wanna talk to her instead? She's the one speaks English."

DeLuca shrugged. "*Artemis* IntairOp speaks a couple of Luxan languages. You need this lovely lady here. Her and this delightful gent." He jabbed a finger at the cleanshaven man. "Make 'em crack open their own damn bulkheads and deck plates. But watch 'em close, yeah?"

"I know my job, ya goddamned shippy," she said, affecting a cheeky smile.

"Hilarious." Still gruff, he paused his comms so only she and Jeng could hear him, and allowed a little warmth to enter his tone. "Badillo and Badawi don't think you two are up to the job. You are. But you're new, Jeng. And Westie, you're young. Just make sure these assholes don't get tricky on ya."

He propelled the cuffed man into the airlock. The man tripped on the discarded helmets as he moved forward and hesitated as if finding his balance, peeping back toward his comrades. There was something in the lines on his face, in the whites of his eyes. Fear, Westermann thought. No, more than fear. *Terror*. She frowned: sure, the idiot was in a universe of trouble, but the depth of that emotion seemed out of place.

She shook off the curiosity as DeLuca barked at the man, shoving him again. "Get movin', puke stain!"

Westermann turned to Jeng. He had his rifle snapped to his chest and his helmet in his hands—and he was breathing through his mouth.

Westermann took his helmet, tossed it into the airlock, then sealed the door between it and the passage. "Leave your bowl here. Help me with this."

Between the two of them, they cuffed the remaining pair of detainees with their hands in front of them. She asked the woman, "You're the captain?"

"Ya."

"Name?"

"Haas."

"Captain Haas. And him, he's what and who?"

She glanced at her comrade. "Pilot. Stepka."

"And I bet he speaks enough English to understand me fine. That true, Pilot Stepka? You understand me?" The man blinked at her. "I reckon you do. I shouldn't have to say this to you idiots, but it's procedure. So. This star system is off limits to all but DCHC military and approved scientific personnel. Your ship and crew have violated an established Exclusion Zone, and you are therefore under arrest. Your ship is impounded under Section 73 of the Trade and Quarantine Act. You'll have your chance to plead your case in court, but we expect full cooperation from here on out. There are things you can do to reduce the seriousness of the penalties you're facing. You understanding me so far?"

Stepka stared, giving her nothing. But Captain Haas nodded. She said, "Most."

"Good. Illegal drugs have already been found aboard. Any *more* contraband here, we're going to find it. Only question is how long that takes. One of the things you can do to reduce the penalties you're facing is to make our search short and easy. Another thing that'll help you is explaining why you're here. What the hell did you want from the planet that gave PBT virus to the universe? I mean, anyone with half a brain knows there's been a military blockade at this leappoint for thirty years." She said this last part to Jeng who'd been watching her performance keenly.

"Common knowledge," he agreed.

"We good cargo peoples," Haas piped up again. "We do da true tings, da good tings, not da bad tings. Some udda person put da drugs here. You keep da drugs. You keep da computer data. But you please let us go now so we fix da ship, and go at Bona Vista, and make pickup dere. You look in computer data and you see we have da invoice for Bona Vista, for carry da cargo from dere to Pollux."

Westermann fought against a surge in frustration, fought against the heat that rose in her chest, against the desire to slap Haas the way she'd seen other PKs slap smugglers and scavvers. In seven hours, the transport ship would be here to take on its final complement of FTL passengers. And it wouldn't loiter long.

A hand dropped onto her shoulder, startling her, snapping her out of her thoughts. Jeng offered her the kind of reassuring wink she'd given him on the skiff, then took over the conversation. "Captain Haas. Tell your pilot he's to come with—"

Jeng never got to finish his sentence as a new comms signal blared in their speakers.

Artemis's Executive Officer said, "Boarding Team, priority task for you. Immediate check on their comms log for an FTL transmission that went out shortly after they arrived."

Westermann frowned at Jeng.

In-speakers, Badawi's voice replied, "An *FTL* package?"

"Confirmed," said the XO.

"Who are they sending to?"

"Exactly. We've tried deciphering it over here and it's just babble."

"That's 'cause they speak Pollux-Dutch," Westermann said.

"No," replied the XO. "It's actual gibberish. Just nonsense code. Check their keystrokes and see if there's a text record pre-encryption."

"Copy that," Badawi said.

"Or we could try asking them," said Westermann. Haas's eyes had widened a little as she'd overheard the conversation. She'd understood it fine.

Jeng asked her, "You commed someone?"

Haas glanced at her pilot and frowned. The man was actually trembling now, and staring at the floor.

Westermann's grin came back: the one bright side of a job like this was making mutts like these two squirm. "Seems like we're onto something good."

The Polluxan captain's shoulders drooped as she

appeared to come to a decision. "I get comm data for you." She jerked her head in the direction of the cockpit. "You take me dere, I help you."

"You'll cooperate?"

Haas nodded.

"Well, then. After you." She gestured with her rifle. "*Captain.*"

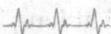

WESTERMANN KNEW what the cargo runner looked like from the outside. The dog team had reviewed long-range imaging before departing *Artemis*. And over the past few years, she'd boarded a dozen similar vessels in orbit over Centauri or out at the Thesian and Caultan leappoints.

The design was common and simple: a long, rectangular block with exhaust nacelles poking out one end and a stubby cockpit compartment the other. From outside the ship, the cockpit looked like an amphibian's head. And being tapered and relatively short in length, it wasn't built for comfort any more than Westermann's assault skiff had been. And no roomier.

She made Jeng wait outside. The low doorframe forced her to stoop as she pushed Haas inside ahead of her. The two women now stood on a two-by-two-meter deck plate, a kind of foyer deck behind the operation stations. The cockpit hull was transparent all round: Westermann hoped it was composed of clearsteel rather than glass, since the vessel's shields were currently powered down. Beyond the shallow foyer plate, two open crew "nests" were stacked one above the other, both accessible via short ladders. The floor of the top one sat a meter higher than the foyer plate, while the bottom one lay a meter-and-a-half lower. Each had room for a single crewer—*just*. She didn't think she'd be able to squeeze into them, especially in her suit. Badawi was shorter than her and he'd managed it. Cool fresh air caressed her face, providing relief from the stink of the passageways, flowing steadily from a vent set into the thick plate that separated the two nests.

Badawi had folded the pilot seat into the decking so he could kneel by the helm console. The techjacker's helmet lay by his right boot with his gloves poking out of it. His fingers pattered away at panels. He turned his head enough to register the newcomers in his peripheral vision. "Who's with you, Westermann?"

"The lovely Captain Haas. Here to retrieve that messagepack she sent out."

Without further word, Haas took the short ladder down into the lower nest and slipped into its chair.

With his head still half-turned, Badawi raised his voice to carry to the captain. "Haas, you better understand this. I've disabled auxiliary controls to that station down there. Don't even think of blowing an airlock or sealing us in the cockpit or some other shit."

"She's not wearing a suit," Westermann said.

"Still."

"You say I help and I get not so much jail, so I help," Haas growled back.

Badawi tapped away at the helm for a moment, then added, "All right, you have comms access again."

Haas made no further reply and Westermann could no

longer see her face: the material of the cockpit hull didn't reflect anything from inside it.

Badawi swore. "Westie, see if you can get her to give me a translation key for these damn logs too." Voice dropping, he added thoughtfully, "Weirdest code I ever saw. Like maybe someone who doesn't speak ..."

He fell silent. Westermann figured he was thinking of ancient CUSET codes, or PRC ones. Then he went stiff, gasping. The kind of gasp that set Westermann's neck hair prickling.

This time when he turned, he twisted far enough around to catch her eye. *His* eyes were wide. Horrified.

He said, "Another ship just leaped in. And it's *massive*."

Chapter 2: Intruders

"A large proportion of spaceships from the pre-Dark Age era were lost completely and probably forever.

The factors contributing to these losses include: the eventual failure of force-shield integrity/power; asteroid/comet collisions; collisions with larger celestial bodies (including stars, it is believed); collisions with other human-constructed objects and vehicles; or they simply traveled out of their home star system and into the vast gulfs of interstellar space where we will never follow.

From the files and registries that survived centuries of data-rot, we can guess that a small number of vessels ended up in star systems whose own exploration records no longer exist for us to examine ..."

Iverson, Cohan & Kalili, *The Reunification of Human Civilization - a History of Recovery after the Second Dark Age*, Dogstar Press, 2998, page 322

"THAT'S AN OLD PRC CARRIER-GUNBOAT."

This comment came from Jeng, who'd now squashed in beside Westermann to stare through the overhead canopy.

She followed his gaze, swearing.

It was impossible to assess size and distance in the void, but the new arrival *looked* huge. Its patchy green-and-white hull sprouted thruster-modules like buboes, launch bays and turrets like lesions. Many of those turrets already jetted long streaks of blue and white energy in the direction *Artemis* had been when the dog team left it. Fresh out of FTL, the thing wasn't in motion yet, and Westermann was looking "up" at it, at part of its belly and starboard hull.

Eyes back on his panels, Badawi said, "It's at least a half-a-klick long."

"Six hundred, twenty-two meters," Jeng replied, absently.

The damn thing certainly blocked out a huge sweep of the starfield. If Jeng was correct, Westermann figured it must be twice the length of the *Artemis*, itself a capital ship with serious bulk and firepower.

She shoulder-bumped Jeng. "You serious? You *sure*?"

"Oh, yeah. The Chinese made these bastards big."

"How do you know this?"

He continued staring upward, rapt. Incoming fire splattered against the carrier-gunboat's shields. "I've always been a spaceship nerd. Loved these old-times

Chinese types. They were crazy good. Never thought I'd *see* one for real. They're all meant to be lost."

Overlapping comm-chatter on Westermann's collar speaker competed for attention with what Jeng was saying. DeLuca and the skiff pilot hollered at *Artemis*. *Artemis* hollered at the skiff pilot. From the back of the cargo runner, Badillo demanded information. Above her, Badawi hissed curses.

And Jeng kept babbling. "The People's Republic built ten of these in the 2120s. One was on its way here during the Red Star Crisis in 2140, but the crisis was resolved before it saw action."

"Jeng," she said.

"It wasn't here when DCHC explorers rediscovered this system last century. No record of where it wound up. Wouldn't that be weird if this was *that* one?"

"Jeng."

"Can't see how that's possible, though."

"*Jeng.*"

"What?"

"Shut your yap."

"Sorry."

Badawi's swearing and the storm of comms chatter kept echoing her own main concern. That gunboat was a hostile. And she was standing in an unprotected cargo runner, with its shield generators fried by *Artemis*, with its thrusters fried by *Artemis*. With a thin skin of glass or clearsteel the only thing between her and those energy cannons.

She stamped a boot into the deck in frustration. "How powerful *is* that thing?"

"It's giving *Artemis* a beating," Badawi called from above.

"They were very powerful, back in the day," Jeng said. "Whoever found it, I just hope they weren't able to get its main guns up to full strength. They're nine-hundred-years old after—"

More light flashed from the far side of the ship, the upper hull. Westermann said, "They look pretty damn 'full strength' to me. You're saying that's now a *pirate* ship?" The question felt stupid the moment it left her mouth; there wasn't anyone else it could belong to. Unless …

Earth? Couldn't be. Could it?

Light flashed her way. The deck rocked once beneath her. Then a greater convulsion ran through the cargo ship. The starfield outside rolled to Westermann's right, disorienting her, making her clutch at Jeng for balance. But, although the ship now yawed to port, turning slowly, the freighter's inertial dampeners still worked. Arti-grav still worked.

She let Jeng go, straightening her posture with a curse to rival Badawi's. "They hit us?" she asked.

All comms chatter had ceased, she realized, the three suit-collar speakers in the room falling eerily silent.

Badawi shuffled around to face her, the blood draining from his face. Gone was the perpetual sneer. Gone was the cockiness. He croaked, "Not us. The skiff."

"What?" gasped Jeng.

"Surgical laser strike. Must have slashed it open along the flank."

The bang and shudder had been the effect of explosive

decompression, then. Westermann watched the rolling starfield beyond the canopy, saw the carrier-gunship slip out of view. The explosive venting of the skiff's air had nudged the freighter sideways and over, spinning it slowly.

"It's ... They're gone?" she asked. DeLuca. The skiff pilot. *Dead*?

Badawi's only reply was the despairing blink of his eyelids.

Her teeth clenched, her fists joining in. "Bastards. Bloody *bastards*!"

"What ya say about the skiff?" It was Badillo talking now, and Westermann heard his question twice, layered over and upon itself. Once through her speakers, once as his shout traveled down the passage behind her. He was close, hurrying forward. Apart from his question, comms remained silent.

"Hacking doghackers," Badawi said, eyes fixed on the starfield.

Westermann's rifle hung from its strap while she put her fists to the sides of her head. *What the hell do we do? What the hell can we do?*

When the attacking ship rolled back into view, it still spurted blue and white energy in the direction of *Artemis*. Movement around it resolved as tiny shapes rocketing out of the launch bays along its flanks and belly, visible by their drive plumes as they spiraled out on crazed vectors meant to avoid enemy targeting.

"Drones?"

"Fighters," said Jeng.

Within seconds, one of the smaller craft hurtled

31

toward them, no longer a blue drive-flare, now a distinct gliding-hawk shape—if that hawk's wings had been angled slightly forward ...

Sorry, Dad, Westermann thought, not even sure what she was sorry for.

She straightened her back, bracing for a fiery death, wondering if it would hurt—but the fighter veered away without firing on them, vanishing quickly as it accelerated while the freighter continued rolling over.

She blew out the breath she'd been holding. "*God.*"

Passing them up close, the small craft had looked all the more lethal.

"Sparrowhawks," Jeng said, confirming her thought in a rasping voice. He started prattling again, spilling facts very fast. "Changhe Z-22 *Sparrowhawk* orbital interceptors. Used by 22nd century Chinese police and air forces. Minimal shielding. Variable laser and ion cannons. Short-range. But damn, they move well for such old vehicles."

"And it could have blown us to atoms," she snarled, silencing him. "You realize we're completely trapped here, right?" Without waiting for a response, she jammed a gloved finger onto her arm panel, rebooting intership comms. "*Artemis*, please tell us you're doing okay."

A pause. Dead silence on comms for a good three-count, then a terse transmission from the XO: "Shut up, Westermann."

"Bitch," she said, letting the word out before releasing the comm button. She stooped, attempting to locate *Artemis* in the distance, but saw nothing out there.

It's two hundred klicks away, idiot. And that was before it was attacked.

The interdictor had no doubt started moving, angling, presenting different shield arcs toward the incoming particle and laser fire.

A shout and the sounds of a scuffle came from the passage outside, spinning her around to peer through the doorway. Badillo wrestled the pilot Stepka for control of the rifle clipped to his combat suit.

"Oh, shit," she said. In the shock and horror of the gunboat's arrival, with the horror of impending death and the loss of their skiff, she'd forgotten about the two detainees.

Bringing up her rifle, she whipped forward—in time to see Haas raise a stubby handgun from down in the lower nest.

The Polluxan captain fired. Westermann fired. The blue Peacekeeper stun-bolt struck Haas dead center of her face and she crumpled into the space between chair and hull glass. In the same moment, something hit Westermann's ear and cheek, warm and sticky. Jeng collapsed, falling against her and slid all the way down before she could get a hand to him. One of his own hands clasped the side of his neck. Dark blood dribbled through his fingers.

"*Shit*," Westermann gasped.

Her ears rang with the crack from Haas's ballistic weapon. She checked on Badawi, then wished she hadn't. He'd pitched backward to land on his ass with a leg trapped under him, his arms spread, his back to the helm. Blood and bone and brain matter dappled the clearsteel behind him. Westermann saw what had happened immediately: Haas's single shot had sliced through Jeng's neck, ricocheted, and taken out Badawi.

And where had the bullet gone then?

Westermann raised a hand to her own head, slapping at it. The glove came away with a red slick across the palm. A narrow smear. No wound in her head. The blood was Jeng's.

Wordlessly, she snarled and put both hands on her rifle.

Haas had twisted unnaturally where she'd tumbled. She could be dead; she could be stunned. Either way, Westermann wasn't in a mood to take chances. She put two more stun-bolts into the woman, ensuring the Pollux-an's heart stopped for good, then dropped to a knee by Jeng. He writhed and moaned and stared at her with pleading eyes. She called for Badillo, loud.

The snap of another stun-bolt came from the passage. She swung her head that way. Stepka was down, Badillo moving toward her.

He said, "What the *hack* is happening?"

She lay her rifle down, reached into her medkit pouch. "You good, Badillo?"

"Hacker's down, yeah, he's *down*." He met her eyes through the doorway. "What … what …?"

Westermann glanced down into the co-pilot well and saw a hinged datapanel had been levered up to expose a small hidey-hole. "She had a gun, hackdammit. Badawi's dead."

Badillo stood at the door now, leaning through it, seeing the mess. He moaned.

She said, "Help me with Jeng."

With a knee on the wounded man's torso to steady him, she fussed with the packaging on a vacuum-compress. Badillo didn't help, frozen in the doorway, swearing and babbling, leaving it to her to coax Jeng's hand away from his wound so she could seal the compress over it.

"You'll be fine," she told the injured man, stilling him. "You're gonna be fine."

A lie. A desperate lie. She'd seen the wound. In the moment she'd gotten his hand off it, blood had squirted onto her suit. Arterial damage. The clamp-compress could only do so much: if they didn't get him onto *Artemis* real soon …

She pulled a roll of dressing from the medkit pouch and cleaned her gloves with it, wiped her cheek and ear.

Something changed then in Badillo's tone. "Oh, God."

"What?"

He pointed through the canopy at the carrier-gunship which was again in full view.

It took her a moment to understand. "It's stopped firing."

Badillo's turn to slap at his wrist panel. "*Artemis*, come in. Commander Dyman, come in. Commander Dyman."

But the XO did not reply. No one aboard *Artemis* replied.

"We've lost them too," Badillo said. "Have we lost them, too? We can't have lost them, too."

Westermann checked on Jeng. A new pit opened in her stomach at the sight of the blood leaking around the edges of the compress. She pressed the bandage roll to it, lifted his head to wind the cloth around. Jeng made no complaint, his breath coming in fast gasps, his eyes closed.

"We're gonna lose us too, if we don't do something," she said. "Badillo. *Badillo*. Is Stepka alive?"

"What? Who?"

"That Polluxan out there. Is he alive?"

He didn't glance back. "I only stunned him. The bastard. Trying to—"

"Badillo, focus. We gotta revive him and get him in that pilot chair."

A flash of movement above them indicated another fighter passing swiftly in front of the freighter.

Badillo pointed after it. "And get torn apart by those?"

"You wanna sit here and get boarded? Torn apart by pirates."

"Let 'em come." He brandished his rifle at the canopy above them.

"Hacking idiot," she said, making the final circuit around Jeng's neck with the dressing. "Wake the Polluxan up. Get Badawi out of the pilot's nest and get Stepka into it. And get us headed for cover. In an asteroid cluster or anything."

"Don't tell me what to do."

"Just *do* it." She tugged the bandage tighter and clipped it together.

"You're not in charge. You're not a real soldier. You've never even been in a real firefight."

"I was just *in* one, hackhead!"

"DeLuca's dead. Isn't he? Isn't he dead? He's dead, so I'm in charge."

"Fine, be in charge. But get that pilot in his chair."

"Don't tell me what to do. You're only twenty-one."

"Twenty-*two*. Are you seriously—"

"Twenty-two. I'm *thirty*-two. I've had actual combat experience. Me and … and Badawi fought those religious nuts at Kavanagh. We defended Drop-in-the-Ocean from Clan Lobos. What action have you seen? Couple of smuggler punch-ups above Centauri, that's all."

He shut up then. Because she was up in his face with a hand latched onto one of his suit pouches. He'd been bowed there, stooped under the low doorway. When he tried to pull away from her, his head cracked against the steel frame and forced a whine of pain.

"I'm seeing action *now*," she snarled. "I'm stuck right in the hackdamn middle of it. You see that corpse in the co-pilot's nest? Yeah? Well, I did that. Me. Now, I'm trying to think of ways to make us safe. And all I'm getting from you is questions, cussing, and more hacking bullying, like the weak flegger you are. You wanna be in command? Start by controlling *yourself*."

She held him in place, bowed within the doorway. Staring up at her from this awkward position, the earlier bluster seeped from his expression. He managed to say, "Uh…"

"Yeah, 'uh'," she mocked, then took a step back, releasing him and pulling another bandage roll from her medkit. She slammed it into one of his hands. "This is to put around Badawi's head."

"Wh …?"

"To keep what's left of his brains inside." The bluster went out of her too then. "And cover his eyes. For … you know … dignity."

37

"Right." He stepped inside.

She let him squeeze past, then went out into the passage to see if Stepka had survived his close-range stunning. He had to be roused so he could fly.

Only problem was, Stepka was gone.

Chapter 3: Stepka and Badillo

"In the mid-22nd century, the second planet in the Shin-tai-yung star system was given the name Red Star by its original Communist Chinese claim-holders. Today, the planet is renamed Zuchola (properly, 诅 咒 了 pronounced "Zoo-*cho*-lah").

Zuchola is widely arid but would be perfectly habitable for humans if it weren't for the sinister part it played in our history.

In the mid-22nd century, the world was the source of the catastrophic PBT virus pandemic which devastated humanity's space settlements. Therefore, today's Confederation Parliament agrees: the star system should remain closed to new colonization, to tourism and to commercial exploitation. The only human habitation permitted on-world is a modest set of permanent research posts established during 2978-82.

Further out in the system, a border interdiction fleet has been stationed by the entry point ("leappoint"). It was established in 2971 to prevent visitors from accidentally (or purposefully) releasing further alien viruses from this system. The exact numbers and composition of this fleet is not on public record."

Iverson, Cohan & Kalili, "The Reunification of Human Civilization - a History of Recovery after the Second Dark Age", Dogstar Press, 2998, page 504

WESTERMANN FOUND the scrawny little bastard in one of the cabins.

Like most compartments on deep space haulers, the bunkroom was economical. A rectangle of empty floor. A double set of narrow bunks along the left wall. A storage closet set within the back bulkhead.

When she came to the door, Stepka was standing with his back to her and the closet door held open. "Hey, *tualedna oostee*," she barked. It was the only Polluxan insult she knew.

Stepka wheeled around so fast, he lost his balance and tumbled against the bottom bunk, then to the floor. Still janky from his stunning, Westermann supposed. She didn't care if he was.

"Up!" she ordered.

But he stayed right there, cowering, his cuffed hands covering his face. "Not me, not me. I no hurting you. I not bad man."

"Oh, you speak English now, huh?"

"I not da bad man, okay? Please, not shoot me."

"Right. You don't want me to shoot you. But you were happy to try for Badillo's rifle so you could shoot him.

40

Get the *hell* off the deck, you midgy little slime, right now."

He scrambled upright and swayed there with one hand gripping the top bunk and the other dangling from the attached cuff. His left eye twitched and a fresh bruise bloomed on the cheek below it. Badillo's stun shot had grazed him, then. The way Haas's shot had grazed Jeng.

She twirled a finger toward the ceiling, the universal signal among spacers that meant *out there in the vacuum.* "Who *are* those guys? And don't say you don't know."

Stepka swallowed. "Dey make me do this. Or dey killing child. My child."

"They have your children?"

"Dey killing child ven I don't help dem."

"*When* you ...?" She remembered then: in Germanic languages like West Centauran and Pollux-Dutch, *ven* meant *if.* "If you don't help them? One child? Two?"

"One."

The dirty *fernatz* was probably lying, but it'd be hard to hate him if it was true. Her anger came off the boil and down to a simmer. "I asked you who they are."

"Dey pirates."

Not Earth, then. As if they would be.

"Xerxians? I never heard of Xerxians in a big ship like that. Most capital ships were lost in the Bad Times. And Confederation worlds found the ones that weren't."

"Dey ... uh ..." He released the bunk to beat his fists against his head a few times. It seemed to jog loose the English words he wanted. "Dey saying dey old Xerxes-Scottish people. Dey have, uh, colony some place vee never knowed of. Dey leave Xerxes planet one hundred years befores and den hiding and fighting dee udda pirates after dat."

"Jesus," she said.

He went on, "Two years befores, I working on ship dat only flies in da Pollux system. No FTL. Just in da system. One of dese ships catch us out dere in da end of da system."

"*Edge* of the system," she corrected distractedly. "Out near a leappoint, yeah? What then?"

"Dey say 'You do verk for us.' W-work, sorry, not verk. My English. I not spake it much. Dese pirates say you do work wid us or we your child will killing."

She still had her rifle on him. She didn't lower it. "If that's true, I have zero reason to trust you, do I? You'd sell me out in a heartbeat." This, he didn't appear to understand. She sighed. "You okay to fly?"

"Fly?" He shrugged, his expression forlorn. "You breaking our ship. And ven we try to move, da pirates, dey catch."

"But you *want* 'em to catch us. Don't you?" She rattled the rifle.

"Want dem catch us? N-no. *No!* Please: you save dis ship. Please you save me. Please you get me to my child. Ven you can helping me hide from dem, den we all go away from here maybe and stay living and I see my child and you see your ... people you loved."

Dad.

"All right, all right, all right."

He was getting worked up, his already-poor English pronunciation and grammar becoming almost incomprehensible. She waved him to silence and demonstrated taking a deep breath. It was only half for him: she was having trouble staying calm herself.

Artemis was gone. Before they could get the freighter moving and hide it somewhere, they'd have to send a distress signal out-system first. The message would bounce from FTL relay to FTL relay for twenty-six hours until it reached the Golan Naval Base where the *Reconcile*-class cruiser *Valiant* was currently stationed, servicing this region of spacelanes. Twenty-six hours for the distress signal to reach Golan and another twenty-six at least for the *Valiant* to power up and make the leap-journey in.

At least, she thought.

The *Valiant* was *much* bigger than the *Artemis*. And it had to be in better shape than a nine-hundred-year-old gunship. It would kick that pirate ship's ass all the way to Sunday. But it would only do Denise Westermann any good if she survived the next fifty-two hours.

At least.

A string of possible sheltering places raced through her mind. The supply ship—still out there somewhere? The various asteroids and debris in this system? The emergency refuge base on one of Zuchola's moons—?

The refuge. If they could get *there,* if they could survive long enough …

If Jeng can survive long enough.

"You know any medicine, Stepka?"

"Medicine? Yes. I fly and I also da ship … *medic* is da word?"

"Medic *is* the word. Come with me." She stepped back and beyond his reach as he came outside on shaky legs.

They stood now in the crew deck's starboard passageway, a corridor split halfway along by a fire-door, a seal-able door-hatch meant to contain fires, sure, but also loss of atmos from hull breaches and so on. She'd had to pass through it to get to Stepka's sleeping cabin, which was aft-side of that hatch. She waved her rifle toward it and the pilot trudged that way.

Following at his heels, she said, "You chubs are working for these pirates, huh? You leaped in first, tested the waters, sent them a signal saying, 'The water's fine, come on in.' Then you sat back and waited for them to come and atomize us. What I don't get is why they haven't blown *this* ship up." She dumbed it down: "Why don't they boom-boom your ship?"

"Dis ship not shooting dem."

"Or they wanna keep it, maybe? It belongs to them, maybe?"

He gave a quick, breathy sigh, stepping through the fire hatch. "I hope dey don't wanting dis ship."

Her turn to step through. "If they don't, want it, asshole, they'll blow us outa the void. No reason not to. Can't leave data about themselves. I mean, they've survived this long without anyone in the Confederation knowing about 'em." She scratched at an eyebrow. "At least, *I* never heard of 'em."

The higher-ups might.

"Maybe dey taking dis ship inside dere ship. We can hide, den we getting away later. But, you want me fly, we fly okay. You my boss. But ven we fly *now*, dey catching us."

"Then you show me how to fly this well enough to dodge 'em while you fix the leapdrive and shields."

44

He stopped dead and turned apologetic eyes upon her. "No no. I don't fix der leaper. Captain Haas da fixer. You ask Haas fix der leaper."

"Can't really do that, fella," she told him as she shoved him lightly forward.

He peered back at her, expression questioning. Then his brow smoothed with understanding, his shoulders drooping. "Oh."

They passed the now-sealed door to the airlock she'd entered through only half an hour ago—or was it not even that long ago?—and she made him pause while she took a glance through the small window. The helmets that had been inside were missing, no doubt sucked through the outer airlock hatch before it slammed shut after the skiff lost atmos. That outer hatch had no window, so she couldn't see anything of the skiff. But a datapanel beside her said a vessel was still locked on out there.

What's left of it, she thought.

She had to swallow a couple of times before she could tell Stepka, "Bastards'll have to board us from the port lock. Maybe through one of the holds. If they board, they'll kill Peacekeepers. If they board, I'll put you in Badawi's suit so they think *you're* a Peacekeeper. You get me?" She slapped her suit. "I'll put you in one of these. Pirates kill me, they kill you too. Understand?"

He replied in a whimper of Pollux-Dutch.

As they approached the final stretch of the forward passage, Stepka suddenly stumbled to a halt. She collided with his back. What she saw over his head and shoulder wrenched a groan from deep within her …

Blood slicked the deck in a broad trail from the cockpit

doorway to where Badawi's body lay along and against a passageway bulkhead. Badillo had wrapped a bandage around his eyes as instructed. The Creep himself sat beyond his dead buddy's head, his suited legs stretched in front of him, head hanging down. The soles of his dark boots shone from stepping in puddles of gore. The other side of him lay Jeng, the noog's neck dressing drenched with arterial blood.

And Badillo had wrapped a bandage over Jeng's eyes.

Oh, no. Oh, God.

Westermann took hold of Stepka's shoulder and spun him into a bulkhead. The impact released an invisible cloud of halitosis and body odor—and a squeak of fright.

"You did this, you sonofabitch. You and your—"

"They're coming," said Badillo, interrupting her, climbing to his feet with effort. "I saw it from the cockpit." His helmet twisted back that way. "A pretty big shuttle. Bigger'n ours. Musta launched the moment they torched *Artemis*."

Badillo's gaze fixed on a bulkhead, his face blank. His arms hung limp by his sides.

She gaped at him. "*Hey!* Hey, *Creep!* Snap out of it."

His eyes slid her way and seemed to focus like twin ranging lenses deciding on a target. "Really thought I'd die an old man, Westie. With a sweet pension and a bunch o' girlfriends on different planets."

Realizing she still had hold of Stepka, she released him—"Do *not* move." —and faced Badillo, advancing on him. "You're not going to die."

He snorted. "We both are."

"Badillo—"

He jerked his head at the ceiling. "In two minutes, we'll hear the clunk of the upper hold bay doors opening. It's a big shuttle and it doesn't look like it'd dock with a small airlock. They'll have to land up there. Another four minutes to get it inside and get the bay doors shut, and repressurize the hold. Maybe as much as ten. Doubt it, though. That gives us ..."

Badillo's eyes went wide in the same moment Westermann caught the scuff of boots on decking. She swung around to see Stepka fleeing down the passageway again.

"This *asshole!*"

She took a few steps after him, then stopped, hesitating.

"Go," Badillo told her, emotion returning to his voice.

He was right, of course. There were other problems, but the pilot could be trying to reach a weapon. The same way Haas had. Westermann picked up the pace, racing after the Polluxan as fast as her suit would allow her.

Stepka reached his cabin a dozen meters ahead of her. As he vanished inside it, he shouted a word. Pollux-Dutch maybe. Or some other language. Or nonsense. She didn't catch it. When she came through the door, he was stepping into the closet at the back of the room. Into it— and *sideways*, vanishing before she could think about firing on him. She led with her rifle as she leaned over the missing closet floor. A crawlspace a meter wide and high ran below this deck. The entire cubby *interior* was missing. His shout had been a voice command, causing the closet to whip sideways into the bulkhead and reveal this access space.

Thumbing her comms on and locking them there, she told Badillo, "Target's in a bolt hole."

"Well, get after him." His voice only came from her suit speaker, not from the corridor outside. He hadn't followed her.

"You *serious*?"

She poked the rifle with its camera facing the way Stepka had fled—then cursed herself for an idiot. Her helmet HUD was long gone, and with it the weapon's camera feed. Stepka hadn't fired on her, though. But if he'd retrieved a weapon and was lying, waiting for her ... the guy was definitely antsy enough to shoot the instant her rifle had appeared.

On the move, she thought.

Scuttling around the ship's tight spaces like the roach he was.

Badillo snarled at her. "Can *you* fly this ship? That's right: you can't. Only *that* asshole can now."

She could hear him outside now, approaching fast. Flicking off her comms, she shouted into the corridor. "Oh, so we're leaving? We're *not* gonna die now?"

"Just get him outa there, Private!"

Swearing, she braced against the closet and considered blind-firing a stun pulse into the crawlspace, but who knew what pipes and whatnot were down there. Triggering the rifle's flashlight, she peeked into the crawlspace, staring along her weapon. The flashlight beam brushed Stepka's head and shoulders before he vanished feet first through a hole in the duct floor. "Sonofa—"

"Get it done," Badillo snapped from the cabin behind

her, startling her. She twisted around, but he was gone again, his footfalls headed aft.

"Sir yes goddamn sir."

Rifle first, Westermann clambered into the duct. Even with all its pouches, her suit wasn't a full-vacuum e-suit, so there was enough space to move as she pushed her rifle ahead of her, crawling as fast as she could to where Stepka had disappeared. Her flashlight revealed a chute, a three-meter straight drop through the lower hold's ceiling. Another meter past the end of the chute, a steel surface, flat, unadorned, non-reflective—a cargo container's roof.

Behind her came the sigh and clank of the closet reinserting itself, blocking her retreat. Stepka remained out of sight, but she could hear the little shenty turd scrambling around down there. Hand holds had been cut into one side of the chute, but they'd be too thin for her gloved fingers. However, with her suit's bracing at knees and ankles, a four-meter freefall wouldn't injure her. Even so, she clipped her rifle in front of her with the flashlight on and braced her hands and boot-edges against two sides of the chute. And slid down.

Hitting the next surface, she tucked and rolled, coming up on hands and knees, head swiveling. This was the lower hold, all right, the air against her cheeks as cold as a dead man's fingers, the compartment's strip-lighting dispelling enough gloom to show her that she knelt two meters from an open hatch in the top of the cargo container. Two cuffed arms snaked out from inside, trying to get enough of a grip to pull it back in place.

Oh no, you don't!

She rushed him, jabbing his hand with her rifle muzzle, causing him to cry out and let go, withdrawing. Westermann followed him in, sliding through the open hatch, expecting to drop three or four meters, but hitting floor much earlier, she grunted as she folded and toppled sideways. The new area was a mere meter-and-a-half in height. Bouncing up into a squat, she found herself inside a smuggling cubby which appeared to run the length and width of the container. It stank as bad as the rest of the ship, the air thick. Soft yellow light emanated from a lumen-strip laid across the middle of the bare plastic floor. Stepka was shuffling to one end where a wide datascreen depicted the feeds from four cameras spread around the ship. He remained unarmed and nothing lay near him that might conceal a weapon.

Westermann turned her head the other way.

And found herself staring into the wide eyes of a child.

Chapter 4: Hidey-Hole

"'CUSET' was technically the name of a legal document, the *Corporate Union Space Exploration Treaty*. But in the early 22nd century it also become the default name for the space-based civilization spawned by the various corporations comprising the (non-Chinese) Corporate Union.

'PRC' refers to the more modest attempts at space colonization by the then Earth nation, the People's Republic of China ..."

Iverson, Cohan & Kalili, *"The Reunification of Human Civilization - a History of Recovery after the Second Dark Age"*, Dogstar Press, 2998, page 27

WESTERMANN GASPED. "That's ... He's ... You got your *kid* here? *Here*?"

From over by his datascreen, Stepka made insistent gestures, urging calm, urging quiet—then urging her to seal the hatch above her.

She ignored his gesticulations. "Why's he here?"

"Safe."

"Safe? *Safety?*"

"I keep him hided from da pirate bastards."

"You—?"

Too much was happening, too many crazy things piling on top of each other. Westermann had to take a long, deep breath—and then another, letting them out slow—calming the pounding in her chest. Now it made sense why he'd run—twice. Stepka wasn't a coward. He was …

He's a dad. He's like my *dad. Just doing what he can for his kid.*

"Goddamn it," she muttered and got the hatch sealed before turning her attention to the child.

The boy.

He wilted under her stare and shrank away, pressing into the corner he'd been crouched in. The kid was small. Because Pollux was still a pretty impoverished place, she couldn't peg his age. On Centauri, a kid who looked like him might be as young as eight standard years old. On Pollux, he might be twelve. He wore his hair long and unbrushed. Dried snot rimmed one nostril.

The bare floor had some give in it, spongy with some kind of noise insulation, she guessed. And it was gritty with food crumbs. The stuffy air, low ceiling and hard steel walls caused Westermann to flashback for a moment. When she was nine, she'd fallen into her father's wool tank, and had to wait a while for him to come find her and, sure, bawl her out for playing there and being careless. At first, she'd been happy to make mounds of the leftover shenty wool and roll in them. Increasingly, she'd grown anxious as the day dragged on —and had felt grateful the tank had rust holes to keep the air fresh.

This hidey-hole had no airholes. It had some atmos cannisters and a large recycler running quietly in the corner near the boy. And it stank, all right. Despite the recycler. The cause for that had to be the sealed toilet-bucket to the boy's left.

"Jesus," she muttered.

By the air recycler sat an unsealed food bin with ready-to-eat meals stacked inside, and empty packets piled outside. On the floor, in front of the kid's toes, a tablet lay face up, powered up, its screen depicting the frozen image from a flight simulator game.

Hunched and with her shoulders brushing the ceiling, Westermann shuffled over to Stepka. "I get it, okay? I get why you ran."

Her left glove had access-triggers for the electronic locks on the pilot's handcuffs. She gripped one of his wrists, and pressed a thumb to one cuff, then the other. When they snapped free, he offered her a weak smile of gratitude.

"Don't be happy yet." She stuffed the cuffs inside a suit pouch. "We gotta get Badillo in here."

Stepka tapped his datascreen. The four vidfeeds on it seemed to originate from cameras fitted into ceiling panels. One on the bulkhead outside the drive compart-ment, directly above the aft passenger elevator doors and looking out. A second above the inner side of the cockpit entry, facing the two pilot nests ...

Oh crap, she thought with a glance back at the kid. *He saw all that shit go down.*

Another camera angled down the corridor between the cockpit and the airlock she'd entered the ship by. The fourth was in one of the holds and Westermann figured it for the lower hold, near their current hiding place.

Stepka pointed to the feed from the elevator landing. On it, Badillo stood stock still before the lift doors with his face raised to the ceiling, probably listening to the bangs and clanks of the shuttle's arrival.

The pilot asked her, "You want *he* in here?"

"Correct."

"Okay. He come quick to da lower hold, den he climbing on top here and come in like we comed in."

"That's the plan." She lay her rifle by her boot and away from him, realizing her comms were locked on still. "Hey, dogface? You hear all this?"

Onscreen, Badillo stretched his neck side to side, easing out cricks. "You found that scav."

"In a hidey-hole. Lower hold. Get your fat ass down here and I'll guide—"

"Negative," he interrupted her. He sidled to the junction of the portside passageway and the elevator landing, turned to face the lift, and took a knee.

"What the hell are you doing?" she demanded, as ice water trickled down her spine.

"What I signed up for."

"Bein' a moron?"

He actually laughed. "Something like that, yeah."

Gritting her teeth, she checked the time on her suit.

"Badillo, by your timing, their shuttle's in the upper hold now."

"It's there. I felt the shudder of the bay doors opening through the decking."

"So, why ya kneeling there like an asshole?"

His head whipped up, searching. "You can see me? Where's the cam?"

"Shut up and get down here."

"I'm ranking PK now, powderpuff. I told you."

Westermann took a moment to glance at Stepka and his kid. They hadn't moved, eyes wide and fixed on her.

"Badillo, say you take down *all* this contingent. They'll send another one. Or vape us from distance, like *Artemis*."

The Creep didn't reply as he lowered himself into a prone position on the deck, keeping most of his body behind the corner bulkheads and in cover from anyone exiting the lift. Being right-handed it allowed him to aim his rifle easily that way.

"Hey, butthole," she barked. "I'm talking to you!"

"Westie, I got my head back in the game now. This is bigger than us; these mutts're planning something real bad here. So, here's how it's gonna roll. I take a few of 'em with me, but leave enough so you don't get vaped."

"Hacking—"

"*You* remain secure with that scavver. He knows something. You find a way to get him and you outa here and onto one of our vessels. You get them the intel on this. Coz I can't, and *Artemis* can't."

Westermann growled with such intensity, Stepka had to murmur reassurances in his language to his kid. At least, it sounded that way. With the translator program paused in her suit, she'd missed the content.

"Badillo," she said into her collar mic, "you're a scumbag, you're a creep, and I hate your guts. But I'm not hiding while you commit suicide by pirate."

Another chuckle from the man onscreen. "Yeah, I'm an asshole, all right. But I'm a Peacekeeper, too. And you know the unwritten law: experienced guys watch out for inexperienced guys."

"I'm not a guy."

"You know what I mean."

"And I'm not inexperienced."

"When it comes to this, yeah, you are."

"But—"

"That law also includes *younger* grunts. And that *is* you, Westie. Plus," he went on before she could object any further, "you need to do what you're ordered to do. Your orders are: make it through this alive, find a way off this tub, protect the researchers at Zuchola, do something for our people on the supply ship, report all this to people who can, you know, rescue me after these chubs capture me."

Damn this.

What he proposed was horrific. No one would be inclined to capture him. He would die. And she'd be alone. Westermann spun away from the screen and planted herself on her ass, knees up, head in her hands. She fought against a rising panic, the sense that this box was leaking atmos and she had nothing to breathe.

Denise Westermann had been raised on a ranch with her sister and her cousins always around, with a constant stream of itinerant Centauran or Thesian workers camped outside her parent's homestead, where loads of people saw what color scanties you hung out to dry.

After her school years, she'd moved to Grace City, into an inner urban block where she could hear her neighbors' fights through the walls. She'd joined the Peacekeepers partly to get away from all that—only to be jammed into shared bunkrooms and shower blocks ever since, crowded by other Marines and shippies, unable to fart without someone knowing about it.

She had never been alone before. And it terrified her, the fear pressing an invisible hand against her ribs, tightening her throat.

But what Badillo proposed made absolute sense. She'd forgotten the couple dozen other Confederation citizens still alive in this system. And he was goddamn right about reporting and intel.

She turned her head to the screen again, found enough breath to tell him, "I don't get why you can't hide, too."

Onscreen, he glanced at the roof, hearing something she didn't. He said, "If they don't find anyone alive, they'll wonder who killed Haas. Coz the two dead Peacers up front sure didn't do it."

"Hack this," she whispered.

"Tell my folks I love 'em?" he asked.

She found the ghost of a smile. "Not your wife?"

"Nah. She wouldn't believe it." He wriggled around on the floor and steadied his rifle. The landing area before the lift was twenty meters wide—most of the width of the freighter—and four deep. Both the port and starboard side passages ran into it. The camera was fixed above those elevator doors, looking down on it and away from it, but she knew there were hatches either side: hatches to systems compartments, a hatch into an emergency ladder-well. Badillo could have tucked himself inside one of the systems compartments and ambushed the pirates as they arrived. It's what she figured she would have done.

But then, she wouldn't be letting herself get taken like he was.

He said, "Comms silence, now, Westie." Then the faint background warble of his audio signal cut out.

"Damn," was all she could think to reply before she cut hers too.

She felt a moment's comradeship with Stepka, fidgeting beside her. If his story checked out, he'd been caught up with these mystery pirates as unexpectedly as she had.

And with his son at stake ...

Settling in to watch the four vidfeeds, she checked on the boy in case he'd moved. He hadn't. And he was about to witness even more violence onscreen ...

So the hell am I, she thought.

"Why is he here?" she asked the pilot.

Stepka scratched at his throat, and it took her a few seconds to get that he was miming her suit's collar speaker. She unpaused the translator prog and made a *go-ahead* gesture. He began speaking in Pollux-Dutch.

Gentle AI-tones prattled in Confederation English from Westermann's collar: "When we were preparing to leave the pirate base, I smuggled him out. I put him in here because I was planning on stealing the ship. When the pirates and Haas got busy on Zuchola. Then I would get us away to Theseus or Oceana."

"Jesus. So, why they go Zuchola?" She decided to keep the English simple since the prog only ran one way.

"They didn't tell me that."

The boy stirred for the first time, then, coming out of his corner and stabbing a finger at the datascreen, he gasped in English, "Look!"

Westermann looked.

Badillo's vidfeed flashed and flared with weaponsfire as he sent a trio of kill pulses in the direction of the elevator. He ceased immediately, still sighting along his weapon.

Did he get someone? she wondered, hoping dead pirates would fall forward from the elevator and into camera view.

Onscreen, Badillo suddenly bucked to his left, tilting to shift his aim toward a different target, a side hatchway maybe. He got off a couple of kill pulses before Westermann saw something dark and hand-sized bounce and roll toward him. Badillo's mouth opened in a wide O, screaming as he tried to curl into cover.

Ice touched her spine once more. Westermann knew there was no cover. Not from this.

The grenade detonated, turning the vision to static for a few moments. Insulated inside this container on the lower deck, Westermann felt nothing, heard nothing. Stepka groaned. The boy asked an anxious question his father ignored.

Forcing herself, Westermann kept her eyes glued to

the vidfeed, waiting until it cleared. And it cleared. And she saw what she saw.

The grenade had been a fragger. Not a stunner. Not a microwaver. Not HE. Shrapnel had scarred the floors and bulkheads around it—and it had hit Badillo in the head, though it looked like he'd tried to curl around and get his armored arms over it. Those arms remained curled, but limp. Blood leaked from beneath them. The rear of the Peacekeeper's head was visible, all peeled skin and pale patches of bone or brain matter amidst the gore. He did not so much as twitch.

"Some bastard tossed it out the ladderwell. He didn't expect it. He should've expected it." It took her a moment to recognize her own voice in her ears, as some part of her mind commentated, analyzed, while the rest of her roiled.

Pirates appeared, then. One. Two.

Six.

Four came from the elevator, two from the direction the grenade had come. They moved outward in pairs, sweeping to port and to starboard, heading into the side passageways, their actions a dark mockery of the ones Westermann's teammates had taken not so long ago.

She'd seen pirates before. On vids, in holos. And live-and-personal on the single occasion she'd transported a prisoner from one place to another. There was no such thing among the clans as a uniform. This group wore a mix of scruffy homespun or cheaply manufactured clothing, along with segments of old CUSET-era body armor. The lack of uniformity applied also to things like age and hair style.

The initial six had passed out of sight now, moving

forwards. They'd been in their twenties or thirties. More appeared, four of them, all younger, adolescents. An older man too, someone DeLuca's age. This one carried himself with the swagger of a squad leader or officer, and he bent over Badillo's body, rolling him onto his side to inspect the compact apparatus regulating airflow and suit temperature. He sported a graying goatee and wore a sleeveless anti-laser vest and a folded yellow bandana around his otherwise shaved head. He sent two of the younger men after the others to sweep the deck, but gestured for the remaining two to stand by the elevator. There they went, bobbing and dancing with adolescent energy.

"Eleven," Westermann told herself. The tallying of hostiles was automatic, reflexive. Wasn't much point counting them, really. Wasn't like she'd be taking them on. No. That had been left to Badillo, while she crawled away to hide.

You left him there to die. The thoughts hammered at her in *Badawi*'s voice. With Badawi's sneer. *It's your fault. You didn't watch Haas. You —*

"Shut *up*," she growled, drawing a confused stare from Stepka.

The earlier panic hadn't left her completely. It remained close by her side, closer than Stepka, itching to get its claws into her, to take over. And it made her angry. Denise Westermann had never let herself be panicked. Not when lost in the woods near her parents' ranch. Not in that damn wool tank. Not in her school days. Not in BASIC. Not on deployment. Not ever. And damned if she was going to panic now …

If she couldn't *do* something useful, she could still *think* something useful.

Locking her grief and fear away behind clenched teeth and the practicalities of the situation, she gave her mind over to the mystery of these people and who they were, forcing her attention onto the bandana-wearing commander as he stooped over Badillo.

Stepka had described this faction as 'Xerxes-Scottish.' Xerxes remained one of two non-Earth worlds yet to join the Confederation. And BASIC geo-history classes had taught Westermann that it had originally been settled by waves of 'nationally homogenous immigrants,' meaning each wave migrated from a *different* Earth locality or country. During the Bad Times, and ever since, Xerxians had clung fiercely to these 'tribal' divides. The various pirate factions attested to that ...

The Spanish-descended factions began as offshoots from the same clan, tough little mutts who'd survived for centuries out in the Xerxian asteroids before getting their modest fleet of old-times ships operational again.

The Filipino-descended clans had come directly from the Xerxian homeworld. They hadn't splintered into offshoots, but had cooperated with each other.

The English- and Vietnamese-descended groups began as slaves before breaking away—but it wasn't clear which other faction had enslaved them, or how.

This rough history taught by the military had come from captured pirates. Who knew how accurate it even was.

All the ones who'd boarded here had so far been *very* fair-skinned, paler than Westermann. They were male, and maybe five had red hair or beards. Stepka claimed this faction was Xerxian, like all pirates, but she'd never heard of one with Earth-Scottish roots who flew around in a big-ass, old Chinese battleship. She'd never even heard the word *Scottish* and wondered at its origins.

"What's their name?" she rasped, finding her throat dry and tight. She ran her tongue around her gums, trying to produce some moisture, irritated now she wore a ship-to-ship combat suit rather than a fully equipped e-suit with water reserves inside it. "The pirates, Stepka. What's their name?"

When the pilot commenced a long-winded reply in Pollux-Dutch, Westermann killed the translation prog. "I'm not listening to this damn thing all day. You're gonna get used to speaking English."

"Okay," he said. "Okay. They name is Shinna Caldones."

"*Shinna Caldones*?" She repeated the phrase a few times, trying it out, then asked, "They're from Xerxes?"

"Later I say you story maybe, yes? Big problems *now* vee having." He murmured something else to his son, offering him a reassuring smile.

The boy had crept closer while Westermann had been distracted. He sat cross-legged on her side of the strip-lighting bisecting the container floor, clutching his tablet to his bony chest. He gave his father's smile a dubious squint before turning his face to his tab screen.

Westermann's attention lingered on him a moment. His pale face had a stripe of food smeared up one cheek. And his eyes burned with wariness, yes, but also intelli-

63

gence. If she was having the worst day ever, what had this poor boy been through as a captive of pirates?

I'll do what I can to get you outa this, kid. Long as your dad cooperates.

"Fair enough," she replied to Stepka. "But you *will* tell me the story later." She returned her stare to the screen and tried to find a comfortable position to sit in her suit.

They watched the various feeds as the pirate boarders wandered the ship. The Shinnas—as Westermann started calling them in her head—paid little attention to the three dead Peacekeepers other than to kick them or make some passing joke about them. This behavior soon made Westermann's jaw ache from clenching it.

The young and scraggly pirates guarding the elevator eventually gathered the courage to defy orders and kneel by Badillo's body. She shuddered to focus on this scene, on Badillo's blood pool and blood spatter, and on the way the youngsters treated his corpse.

These two might have been thirteen or fourteen, only a few years older perhaps than the boy here with her. And nothing like him in size or demeanor. The modern PK pulse rifle was long gone, claimed by one of the first boarders. But there appeared to be plenty more to fascinate them. One pulled a data-pen from Badillo's chest pouches and poked it repeatedly at his damaged head. The other puzzled over the clasps and locks on the Peacekeeper e-suit before figuring some out. Together they began to strip it off the dead Marine.

Westermann had to stop watching, had to change her focus or else she'd explode.

The other roving pairs inspected the crew deck in the

casual, haphazard way of amateurs, picking over it and pocketing items of interest, but not examining anything closely. When two appeared in view of the lower hold's camera, close to finding her hidey-hole, they also didn't take much care in checking everything. They merely tapped on containers, kicked at the one she was in, then moved on and away without suspicion. Briefly, she heard the musical chatter of their careless conversation through the container wall. When this pair later reappeared on a crew deck camera, she relaxed a notch.

On the feed from the cockpit, the commander with the yellow headscarf now chatted with a willowy woman who'd arrived late. She wore patchy body armor and had climbed down into the co-pilot's nest, straddling Haas's corpse without seeming bothered by it.

Westermann pointed to the cockpit feed and asked Stepka, "You got audio?"

He frowned at her a moment. "*Awd*-ee ...? Oh." He flicked at something on the panel. The couple's conversation whispered from a tiny speaker, Stepka smart enough to have the preset at a low volume.

Westermann hadn't expected to understand their language, and she didn't. In any case, it was interesting to hear it: its soft consonants and tuneful rise-and-fall were in stark contrast with the pirates' violent arrival in the star system. A couple of times over the next ten minutes, the two senior pirates were interrupted by others, enough for Westermann to make out names for the pair. Names or titles, possibly. The underlings had called the bandana-wearing guy Braith, and called the lanky female Moree. Or that's what it sounded like to Westermann.

"How many are onboard?" she wondered out loud, knowing her initial count had to be revised. She pictured the various faces and "uniforms" she'd seen wandering the crew deck and the belly hold. She'd seen twelve she was sure of, including Moree. Two or three more might be up on their assault shuttle. A pilot, maybe a medic. "Let's call it fifteen to be safe. Me versus fifteen. And if they take the freighter inside their carrier ..."

Braith and Moree had arranged themselves in relatively comfortable postures, in no hurry to leave. She watched and listened to them talk amiably, calmly—just two coworkers shooting the breeze.

"Why the hell are you here?" she asked their images.

From the briefings she'd actually been concentrating in, the military believed that any pirate factions interested in Zuchola must have already investigated it and lost interest decades before other planets got their crap together. Or, more likely, they were as scared of the place as the Confederation was. They certainly hadn't come here since the Exclusion Zone was created to block the leappoint.

"The way they set this up, they won't need to smash-and-grab," she said. "They can take their time."

If *Valiant* turned up, it could kick that carrier-gunboat's ass, all right. But the damn Shinnas still had fifty-plus hours to screw around before leaping safely out ahead of *Valiant*'s arrival.

Fifty hours. Long time to keep avoiding 'em. Plenty of time for them to keep doing evil crap.

Zuchola was a mere eight hours' sub-light travel from the Exclusion Zone in a fast ship, given its current position relative to the leappoint. The carrier could get there, slaughter the scientists on the research stations, steal a boatload of stuff and get back here with time to spare.

Steal, she thought, scratching her head. What would these sociopathic Neanderthals be after? *Please, Universe, don't let it be PBT.*

The thought should have added a deeper chill to the coldness already gripping her body, but it didn't make a lot of sense. Why would pirates want a superbug when weaponizing it would be as dangerous to them as to anyone else? And *could* they even find it and contain it? She had no idea what "research" the Confederation was conducting on and above the planet. Their scientists conducted it well away from the region the virus originated, that's all she knew. What had happened in that region was a matter of historical record; its location was information anyone could get their hands on. But if there'd been one supervirus down there, who knew how many others the planet was home to? That, after all, was the point of the Exclusion Zone. And maybe of the government's research.

A whole damn habitable planet just sitting there, she thought. *Earth-sized. Grav-normal. Goldilocks zone and everything. And nobody can live on it.*

Stepka prattled something beside her.

She growled, "English, dammit." But he was talking to his son. She added, "Uh, sorry." Then growled again at *herself* for apologizing to one of the guys who'd gotten her into this.

Half-turning from the datascreen, she faced him fully, keeping the kid in her peripheral. The rifle stayed firmly behind her at her heels—and for the first time ever, she wished that Peacekeepers brought handguns onto boarding parties rather than these bulky things. "Listen to me carefully. Try to understand me. We gotta survive for at least fifty hours." She tapped the digital time display on the datascreen, then flashed him all her fingers five times. "Fifty hours."

"I know fifty."

"You know 'survive?'"

He nodded. "Living."

She narrowed one eye at him. "You understand English better than you let on, don't you."

A mild blush, and another nod.

"Goddamn smugglers. Okay. After fifty hours or so, a big Confederation ship comes."

"Fifty is long time."

"Tell me about it. You, me and your boy, we gotta get off this boat. If the pirates haven't torched it yet, it means they wanna keep it. It's a perfectly good ship. They'll tow it aboard the carrier, and I don't want be on *that* when it leaps out. Also, I got people on a supply ship headed out from Zuchola. And people on research stations in orbit and on-world. *Artemis* would've sent 'em warnings, but it'll be a couple hours or more before the supply ship receives those comms, and maybe another four before the messages reach the planet. Meantime, that gunship could already be moving toward them."

It was the first time that last part had occurred to her, and she cursed under her breath while gathering her thoughts.

"To sum up. We gotta get off your ship and alert the

others. *Then* we gotta play cat and mouse till the *Valiant* arrives."

His left eye was squinting at her, and she realized she'd gotten carried away with her explanation.

Sighing, she dumbed it down. "For fifty hours, me boss. Okay?"

He understood that all right. Objections flickered across his face for a moment, but he nodded, accepting it. "But you help my childs."

"*Child*, Stepka. Child. Boy." She passed a hand across her face. "You really gotta learn better Conglish."

FOR A LONG TIME, the Shinnas lugged pieces of equipment out the elevator and through whatever hatches were beside it, out of view of the cams. Fixing the leapdrive and shields, Westermann figured. Stepka viewed this activity with a deepening frown, chewing his lip so hard Westermann started taking bets with herself on how long before it started bleeding.

At the hour-twenty mark, she turned from the screen, opened and closed her eyes a few times and ran through the few stretches possible within the confines of her suit and the hidey-hole. She kept hoping for inspiration to hit, some bright plan like a streamie hero might think up. But all she had were tight muscles, a dull ache in the pit of her stomach, and a parched throat. Once again, she regretted not being in a bulkier, EV model combat suit with its own water supply. Still, she wasn't yet desperate enough to sip from the boy's water bottles, given she had no idea whether or not he washed his hands after using that toilet-bucket.

At least the kid was getting used to her, she thought— or maybe just not spooked by her presence anymore. His name, his father had told her, was Gerrit. A while back, he'd returned to the flight simulator game on his tablet. From what she could see, the prog used Confederation English, so at least someone on this boat was learning it. He glanced at her whenever she changed positions for a new stretch, indicating the wariness was not entirely gone. She pulled out of her stretch to rummage in a suit pouch for the energy bars she'd been issued for the mission. Three of them. She tossed one near Gerrit's feet, then offered another to Stepka. The pilot took it absently.

"They're tasty," she assured them, tearing the end off her wrapper. "Navy actually feed us pretty good out here. Better'n a lot of other postings I've been on." She bit some off and chewed, thinking. "Probably coz they know a posting this boring needs *some* perks or we'd all go loco." She kept eating, and chuckled with dark humor: this posting had just become the least boring thing she could imagine.

For a while now, Stepka had been making a low noise deep down in his throat, as if he had something to say. He'd laid the energy bar aside without eating it, fixating on the screen even though there was no one visible on it currently.

Except for Braith and Moree in the cockpit. The pair now seemed completely disinterested in any ship's data. Probably, they were taking advantage of a quiet place to share some shop talk or flirt. The rest of the pirates seemed to be working in the drive compartment or else they'd returned to their shuttle. She was certain at least six of them remained in the compartments behind the elevator shaft, repairing the ship's systems.

Stepka made the noise again, so she tapped his arm with the back of her hand. "What is wrong?"

"I'm worry."

"Um, yeah. Me, too."

"No. I'm worry about dis." He tapped the screen over the elevator and drive compartment. "I don't thinking dey doing repairs."

"Well, what else are they doing in there? Cooking supper?"

He got the sarcastic tone, if not the meaning. "Listen me. Please. Many parts dey took in dere are not ship parts."

"They probably have their own parts. Probably make 'em for 'emselves and they just look different. Anyway, you said Haas was the 'fixer,' not you."

"Yah, but I know how da parts looking. Most what dey carrying in dere wasn't da modules and other tings we using."

"Then …?" *Oh, God.* "A bomb? You think they're turning this ship into a bomb?" Putting it together, she added, "To ambush whoever leaps in next and investigates."

"Yes, I tink."

"Animals!"

If a ship came in close enough, if the Shinnas somehow harnessed the ship's reactor to make the explosion nuclear, then the resultant EMP and radiation blasts

might weaken even a capital ship's shields badly enough
for debris to pierce as shrapnel.

Stepka said, "I for one week wondering why dey
needing us leaping here first."

"A distraction."

"Maybe dey can't putting a bomb onboard when Haas
and us control da ship. But dey can now. And your ship
sending messagepack before dey destroying it, and dat
message will having data ..."

He appeared to run out of English, so Westermann
finished his thought.

"Data on your freighter, and data on my dog team
being here. And about how damn helpless we all were. So
Valiant comes through and its first priority is to come
check on us."

"Dey want making sure Peacekeepers okay."

"Sounds about right," she growled.

"And—" He swiped the four vidfeeds into one-half of
the screen and brought up a new data window. This one
had raw code running across it. "—see dis?"

She made a *means-nothing-to-me* face at him.

He asked his son a question. Gerrit raised his head
and peered at the screen, then told Westermann, "It's a
comms buoy signature code. Like a transponder code."
And went back to his sim.

Jesus, he has been learning good English.

To Stepka, she said, "Bastards launched an in-system
comms buoy, but the identity marker signature's fake. Or
it's stolen."

Stepka's finger traced a line of code. "Dis a Blood Dog
one."

"They're gonna frame another pirate clan."

"*Frame?*"

She waved off his question. "Stepka, we gotta get off this boat. Yeah, I know, kinda obvious. But we gotta get off and destroy it. Then we gotta hide you and your kid somewhere while I help the rest of my people. No more sitting around on my ass."

Stepka hadn't understood all of that.

But Gerrit had. The boy had put his pad down, watching her keenly. He flinched when she locked eyes with him.

"You speak English, don't you?"

A hesitation, then: "Yes, sir."

She softened her expression. "Not 'sir.' Just call me ..."

Denny? Denise?

"Westie. Or Private. And I promise I'll keep you safe."

"Okay."

"*How* do you know English? School?"

"A bit. When I was little. I learned good English from games." He nudged his tab. "All the geecees speak hard English. You know geecees?"

"I do not."

"Game characters."

"Oh." The kid's *accent* was certainly as thick as his father's, but so far his Conglish was damn good. "Well, hooray for tablet games. Coz your dad and I are gonna rely on your English skills a *lot*."

Movement on the vidfeeds drew her attention: Braith passing the airlock along the starboard passageway, having left Moree alone in the cockpit.

Could Westermann use that? Was it an opportunity?

C'mon, brain. Gimme ideas. Some good ones.

Damn, her jaw really hurt. She'd been clenching it again. She waggled it from side to side, trying to massage the joints where it hinged, but her gloves were too bulky for such a fine task. She unhooked the left one: not much point wearing the damn things now anyway.

"Gerrit," she said. "Translate this for your dad, please. Can he use this datapanel to access all of his ship's data, not just comms data?"

She got the left glove off as the boy translated, and lay it out of the way by the nearest wall, then started on the right one as Stepka hummed to himself, apparently unsure what he'd be agreeing to.

"We won't survive without information," she told him and studied Moree onscreen for a few seconds. The woman appeared to be daydreaming, picking her nose and staring out at the starfield. "If you tap the ship's main servers, will she notice?"

"Do she see me do it?" Stepka said, understanding her just fine. "No. Da helmpanels don't seeing what other, uh, terminals doing around the ship."

When the right glove lay beside its twin, Westermann pointed upwards. "The shuttle. Find out if it's still there. If it is, I want to know its size. Is it short or long range? Who's currently onboard? Is it possible to patch into its data and find out more about the carrier, the big ship?"

Stepka looked to Gerrit to translate that, perhaps because she'd rattled the list off fast.

When he had her meaning, the pilot blew out a breath. "I trying." He turned to the small keypad under his datascreen.

Westermann smiled at Gerrit. "Thanks, my friend. Can you ...?" She was going to suggest he go play his simulator game again. But she noticed his shoulder satchel near his food stores. "Can you put some food in your bag, please?"

He scooted away to comply. Westermann leaned in and startled Stepka by grabbing his arm. Keeping her voice down, she said, "Don't just be 'trying,' guy. You get me that data and get it accurately. Or we're all dead. You. Me. And him. You understand?"

The pilot swallowed with a loud click and stared back at his son. Then he nodded and bent over his keypad with fresh determination written into the lines of his face. "I understand, Peacekeeper. I understand."

Chapter 5: Assault Shuttle

"You can overthink things later.
You gotta survive long enough to do that first."

- Staff Sergeant Judah
Westermann's BASIC Training Instructor

HEAD AND SHOULDERS bowed beneath the container's low ceiling, Westermann unlatched the various fasteners around the upper section of her combat suit. The tight space was a nuisance as she struggled to shuck the damn thing off without knocking against the sides of the box.

Without a helmet, the suit was useless as protection from the environment—and a liability if she wanted to assault that shuttle in a stealthy fashion. Heftier models of combat suit had robust ballistic plating and specialist anti-laser coating. But those suits were used for planet-based police actions, or for when Peacekeepers went on serious away missions from capital ships like *Valiant*. They were designed for prolonged firefights with regional warlords' militias, with terrorists and, of course, with pirates—all tougher opponents than smugglers.

This one simply wasn't as sturdy. Although the military called its material "soft armor", the name was misleading for two reasons: the outer fabric was more *stiff* than *soft*, so it rasped against surfaces and even against itself, making noise—also, the armor component wasn't tough enough for the kind of firefight these pirates might give her. The new inspection team models had armor designed to cope with short, violent, ballistic-weapon encounters. It would protect against a blade, but more than a couple of rounds from a low-yield laser or pulser might punch on through it. It might even rupture if a mere three or four high-caliber rounds impacted within a small area. If she found herself in vacuum, the soft armor would protect her from the absolute zero of space for three hours—but with the helmet on, the idiots who'd designed it only provided it with two hours of air. Even the most ancient of Earth's space missions had more than that, she was sure of it. It was something Peacekeeper Command kept promising to fix. But never did. All up, she told herself, these new outfits didn't deserve the name *combat* suit.

Besides, she no longer needed its user-assist features. Without a helmet and support data from a main ship, she had no HUD.

Dumping herself on her ass, she wrestled the legs and boots off. Gerrit and Stepka had studiously avoided looking directly at her the whole time. Gentlemanly, she thought. Given the amount of gawking she'd gotten from creeps like Badillo over the years, she was grateful for Polluxan manners.

"Can't say I ever tried doing this inside a goddamn hidey-hole before. Oh *yeah*," she added with relief as the first boot came off. She wriggled her bare toes, flexed the foot. "Freedom at last."

Stepka glanced at her, then looked away, distracted by the flow of code in a corner of his screen.

The cargo runner's servers had provided basic sensor and visual data on the pirate shuttle. Enough to know it had a roomy cabin with a large thruster and fuel section, making it likely to be a long-range assault vehicle rather than a ship-to-ship vehicle like her skiff had been.

"Listen," she said to him. "That thing up there. You sure you can fly it?"

"Shuttle, good, yah. Anyting dat flying in space, I can flying."

"Excellent." She started on the other boot. "If I can secure it and get you aboard, we can drop you two at a refuge station and hide you there. There's one on Zuchola's smallest moon."

She had to drop her head a second to hide the mild blush that touched her cheeks. It shamed her to hide a fact from them: there was another refuge station much closer than that, positioned on an ice-rock a mere ninety-thousand klicks outside the leapzone.

But she needed Stepka to land her on the planet.

God. You're actually thinking of going to Zuchola, onto Zuchola. You are completely loco.

The other boot came loose, allowing her to peel off the

ends of her suit legs. Talking slowly, she continued, "The Navy placed the refuge station there for emergencies, like accidents in space. It won't be comfortable. For example, there's no gravmatting, and the native gravity's only about point zero-two of standard. But it'll keep you alive. Soon as a new Navy ship comes close enough—and it will —its transponder signal will trigger an SOS and they'll come get you. You understanding this?"

Stepka and Gerrit both nodded.

"The Shinnas won't inspect a minor target like the refuge station even if they know about it, which they probably don't."

Stepka said, "Okay. I flying us dere to da moon."

"Good. Good."

With the suit completely off, she piled it against a wall and paused to catch her breath. She now wore her steel-gray insulated undersuit only. The undersuit was long-sleeved and long-legged but left her hands and feet bare.

Better for sneaking around.

Also, if she actually got time to pee anytime soon— and somewhere private to do it—she wouldn't need to go inside a combatsuit, and be stuck in a giant diaper for the next two days.

Dragging her rifle over, she checked its charge. A reflex, a procrastination: she'd only fired a couple of shots from it. The chargepack's tiny display read **247** in blue and **98** in red: two-hundred-forty-seven rounds on stun setting, ninety-eight on AP.

'AP,' she thought. *Anti-personnel.*

Anti-people.

Anti-pirate.

"Yeah. Anti-pirate sounds right." She nudged the selector switch forwards. After detaching the baby shenty skull from her combat suit, she clipped its short chain to the empty sight rail along the top of the rifle.

The suit pouches contained a little gear, but she saw no point in taking any of it, having no pockets in her undersuit and nowhere to secure pouches. Gerrit had packed some food and medkit supplies into his shoulder bag and still had room for his tablet. She could cram a spare rifle chargepack in there too, but did she really want a kid carrying *that* around? The idea felt kind of unclean.

Short term, if I need more ammo than this, I'm good as dead anyway.

She could always loot weapons from neutralized hostiles. Which seemed fair, since they'd done the same to her teammates. She asked Stepka, "We estimate fifteen pirates, right?"

"Fiften? I tink dat's right."

"Let's hope. Six of 'em are making the bomb. Their commander guy just went in to help 'em, so that's seven. Moree, the woman, is relaxing up front, still sitting on top of Haas's body, the ... weird ... bitch."

She winced, realizing that Gerrit was quietly translating her prattle including the swearing. His pointy-chinned face had reddened at the word *bitch*.

"You don't need to translate the bad words."

"Okay." The sigh he heaved underlined his relief.

Yeah, I don't reckon I'd enjoy cussing around my dad either, kid.

"That leaves seven upstairs," she continued, focusing. "*If* they're all up there."

When she'd slung the rifle, she tightened the strap so it lay more snugly against her back.

With the element of surprise, I can do this. I can do this.

She moved beneath the hatch. "I'll take point. *Go first,* I mean. You know how to keep quiet, Gerrit?"

"Yes."

"Really, really quiet?"

"Yes."

"Make sure you do. Both of you."

Thin foot and handholds ran up the chute back to Stepka's crawlspace.

Without the combat suit's fat boots and gloves, climbing wasn't so difficult. Stepka was a heavy breathing presence at her feet with the boy coming up after him. Stepka's shoulder bag made soft shushing noises as he scraped it along behind them. She paused a third of the way along the duct to the cabin closet. It was gloomy, but not completely dark, with Stepka holding his son's tab now as a dim flashlight. When the pilot joined her in the crawlspace, she nudged him.

"Ready to open that closet again?"

Light bloomed brighter from the tab screen as the man activated another camfeed.

"More camera," he whispered and showed her his empty sleeping cabin. "No one in dere."

"Open it up for me."

He uttered his magic word and with a hiss and sigh, the closet folded up and away from Westermann, allowing her access into the cabin. On bare feet, she padded to the open door to the passage and snuck a peek outside and both ways. No one. She pushed the door closed without engaging the lock and hissed a summons to the other two. When they joined her, the color had drained from the pilot's face again, perhaps because of the increased possibility of discovery. Perhaps because he was considering something stupid. Like betrayal.

"You're working with *me*, right, Stepka?"

A swallow. "Ya. Yes."

"And you're not going to tell the Shinnas I'm here?"

He understood it without any miming from her, without any translation progs or help from his son. His color returned as genuine anger flushed his cheeks.

"Tell?" he whispered. "I don't tell doze bastard. I don't helping doze bastard anyting."

"That's the correct answer." She patted his cheek.

Loosening her rifle strap and swinging the weapon forwards, she pulled the door back on its hinge. It was Stepka's turn to take point, leading the way ten meters aft toward the captain's cabin. The whole time, Westermann kept Gerrit beside her, hugging the bulkhead while her muzzle swept before and behind them. They entered Haas's cabin without incident. Westermann closed the door, heart pounding. They'd made it. So far.

This room was the same size as the other one, but with a single bunk set higher in the wall to allow more storage beneath it. Someone had dragged a footlocker from under there and left it open. Westermann saw tattered underwear and t-shirts, still-images of farmland, unlabeled holo-discs—and several bottles of hooch. She guessed the Shinnas were planning to loot those later.

Oh, God, I could use some o' that right about now.

"We go here," said Stepka and opened the captain's closet.

"You guys really love hiding things behind closets, don't you?"

He started muttering as he pushed Haas's spare pants, dress shirt and coveralls to the side.

The boy mimed a tight space. "Dada says this ladder tube we must climb is very ..."

"Narrow?" she provided.

"Very narrow. He says your suit had the box-thing on the back and it would get you sticked in there if you wore it, so it's good you took it off."

"Stuck," she corrected, absently. "Stuck in there."

With the cupboard's back wall uncovered, Stepka used two fingers to trace a symbol. A second later, there came a dull pop and the panel slid up and out of view to reveal, as promised, a narrow ladder.

"Nice tech," she said.

There followed more chatter in Pollux-Dutch from Stepka.

As his father led him into the closet and got him onto the ladder, Gerrit translated, "The pirates gave it to us. They said it's old Chinese." He climbed out of sight.

"You next," she told Stepka who already had a foot and both hands on rungs, watching his son.

The cabin door whisked open.

Moree.

The lanky woman stood there, a meter away, swaying on her feet, clutching an empty bourbon bottle the same shape and label as the ones in the foot locker. And as

Westermann fumbled her rifle around, Moree stepped through the doorway and swung the bottle.

Westermann's left elbow rose to meet the pirate's hand. The impact jarred the bottle free, sending it tumbling behind Westermann and bouncing away to her right without breaking. With her left elbow up, her rifle's muzzle was pointed back over her shoulder with the butt angled toward the other woman's chest. By the time Westermann decided to jab with it, Moree was in motion again, left hand against the rifle stock and pushing hard, her long legs surging against the Peacekeeper. Westermann allowed herself one backward step, trying to create space—and Moree took advantage of it, her right arm sweeping under the rifle and snapping forward in a gut punch.

Westermann had expected it, had tensed her abs to absorb it, wasn't really hurt—but the blow was a warning. She was reacting not acting, wrestling for control of the weapon when she should have been putting the other woman down. Shifting balance, she torqued the rifle sharply to the left, breaking Moree's grip on one side before leaning in, attempting to slam the rifle butt into the pirate's scalp.

Once again, her opponent took advantage of the extra space to snap-strike at her body, this time landing the blow on the side of Westermann's left breast. And this one *hurt*!

Westermann's breath snagged in her throat. She almost released the rifle. Almost. Snarling outrage, she dropped her left hand off the rifle, grabbed a fistful of Moree's shaggy hair, forced the woman's head back then slammed her own forehead into her nose. A gasp and a grunt from Moree. The pirate's remaining hold on the gun went slack enough for Westermann to release her hair, snatch the weapon free, then get a bare foot up and against the pirate's belly. Westermann propelled her into the wall beside the door, raised the gun and put an energy pulse into her face. Moree crumpled against the wall, face collapsed like a sink-hole, fluids leaking down onto her shirt, reeking like half-cooked pig fat.

"Bitch," Westermann spat. Not once in the whole scuffle had the pirate spoken—and until the broken nose, she'd grinned drunkenly the entire time. Westermann's teeth were clenched in pain and rage. If Moree had been a man, she would have kicked his body in the balls as retaliation. Instead, she put a second round into the woman's chest.

Locating the cabin door lock, Westermann secured it, then turned to find Stepka crouched frozen in the closet—with a tight grip on the ladder and his jaw sagging open.

"What the hell you waitin' for?"

He startled into action. A few seconds passed before he got high enough for her to follow him into the closet. The moment she was fully inside, the pilot barked down a word, a new word. The panel slid obediently into place at her back.

While he ascended, she pressed her arm against the bruised breast, testing it, and hissed as it caused more aggravation. Maybe poking such a bruise was a dumb idea. Maybe abandoning the combat suit had been a worse one.

"*Bitch*," she snarled at the memory of Moree's corpse

and climbed after Stepka, shallow-breathing the whole way up.

By the time she reached the top of the ladder, the pain from the blow had ebbed just a tad. Stepka and son had already hurried out of an open panel in the deck despite her whispered commands to wait for her. Stepka had lifted the panel on a hinge, flipping it carefully onto the deck outside. She knew the bay doors couldn't open while the freighter registered life signs within the chamber—she and the Polluxans would be fine for the moment without e-suits. Relatively fine.

She eased the top half of her head through, surveying the hold, forcing herself to take deeper breaths, watching her exhalations curl into vapor in the cold air. Stepka had brought her out dead center of the deck. The upper hold was pretty high, and wider than the level they'd just come from, extending out past the port and starboard sides of the crew deck. A heavily insulated bulkhead partitioned it from the stern thrusters and leap drive assembly. Decades of landings had scorched and scored the thick deck plating around her. And the belly of the pirate shuttle sat right above her head—about *a meter-and-a-half* above her head ...

Since most of its lower fuselage was visible from here, she figured "shuttle" might have been the wrong description for the vehicle. Its simple design was akin to the Traghetti-model pursuit runners Foucault had produced forty years back, still in common use around the DCHC. A long personnel carrier built for speed and distance. The thing was two-thirds the length of the cargo hold, meaning its pilot had been damn good at their job. They must have come carefully through those bay doors on a slant, with the shuttle's nose angled down, before leveling out.

And the vehicle was narrow, essentially a conveyance for personnel without amenities such as sleeping berths or galley. Even from beneath, she could tell a third of the vehicle was devoted to an aft thruster module. As Stepka had surmised, someone had built this thing for prolonged journeys within a star system. And with a thruster module that large, it'd be fast.

The shuttle stood upon four narrow skids. On the fuselage between the front skids, she saw twin bulges, a shield emitter and the rounded turret for a modest laser cannon. At the vehicle's nose, a passenger ramp had lowered to meet the deck, blocking the view beyond it.

Stepka and Gerrit were scurrying away from her, keeping low, headed for a tangle of netting secured to one side of the bay. Westermann could forget them for the moment, so she left the access well they'd climbed up, grimacing at the tenderness in her side, creeping on the balls of her bare feet to emerge on the shuttle's starboard.

Immediately, her right big toe caught on something, stinging enough to make her suck air between her teeth. She turned the foot over. Blood beaded where the fleshy part of the toe had scraped over some ragged scoring on a deck plate. Teeth clenched, Westermann mouthed curses. As she padded toward the front of the ship, rifle butt against her right shoulder, every second footstep stuck a little, leaving another spot of blood behind her.

Pressed against the hull as she crept, Westermann wouldn't be visible to anyone who happened to be looking as the cabin windows were a full meter higher than her head. The access ramp had come down from beneath the vessel's stubby cockpit area, like the jaw of a giant animal. Because the nose and pilot windows were still forward of this, she'd be able to enter without anyone seeing her.

Except …

A whiff of acrid stink wafted her way. Tobacco. Someone sat up on the ramp with their back to her, smoking. A male, wearing a sleeveless anti-laser vest plus a dirty yellow bandana, folded and looped around his bald head. The officer who'd been chatting with Moree. He hummed softly in the careless manner of the tone deaf. A cordless earphone covered each ear.

Westermann got her head above the ramp at the officer's back, peering up and into the shuttle's single compartment. She saw the first row of crash couches, and heard the burble of happy conversation from somewhere inside. Two voices, no, three. Men. No one visible. AP rounds were noisier than stun-bolts, but the yickety-yack up there would be loud enough to stop them hearing it. So she lined up and hit the officer in the spine with a single round. Without even a grunt, he flopped forward and over the side, landing with a muffled thud out of sight.

She hopped up, clenching against the sting in her toe, and the complaints from her bruised boob. Weapon up, she ascended the ramp at a fast walk. With the increased height came a clear view along the cabin: five rows of three crash couches each. All empty. Westermann swung one-eighty and backed the rest of the way up the ramp until she was inside and facing the open cockpit area.

Contacts. Four men, not three. Cackling and talking over each other. Standing behind the two pilot seats. Long-muzzled pistols holstered at their hips. No body armor. Hands in pockets or arms folded. All with their backs to her.

And watching a ceiling screen above the pilot windows.

Onscreen, a section of video played on a six-second loop. The high-yield energy-cannon pounding of a Confederation Naval Vessel. The mild blue fizzling of a shield bubble collapse followed by a chain of explosions throughout the ship.

The death of the *Artemis.*

A red haze descended over Westermann's vision. The aches and pains vanished. Her gut turned cold. A new strength flooded her limbs.

"They saw their own death coming," she told the Shinnas in a loud voice. Heads turned with eyebrows raised and mouths hanging open. "Only fair you should too."

She fired, her finger stroking the trigger as fast as she could. Only the guy to her extreme left went for his sidearm, though he didn't clear it from its holster. The group fell in a tangle around the pilot chairs.

A quick head-check confirmed no extras had come out of the shitter cubicle at the very back. She put another round into each man from up close, charring clothing and skin.

The red mist bleached away immediately. Westermann

slung her rifle behind her and returned to the ramp, crouching, listening. When there were no sounds of alarm, she called the Polluxans in, checked on Yellow Bandana, put a round into his torso.

The father and son joined her inside the cabin. She pointed forward. "Help me throw them outside."

As she struggled to get a grip on the first of the dead men, Stepka got his hands under the armpits of a second, looking damned unhappy about it. She'd expected him to make Gerrit stand out of the way, to let the adults finish their gruesome task. But he surprised her by ordering the boy into one of the pilot seats. Once he'd picked his way around the other bodies, Gerrit jumped into the chair and started on preflight checks and system warm-ups.

"Christ," she muttered. "Smart kid."

After the first two bodies were outside, she unclipped the pistol belts from the third and fourth men and lay the belts aside. The long handguns within their holsters were ballistic weapons and heavy, as heavy as they looked.

"For insurance," she told Stepka. He shrugged, not knowing the word.

After the final pirates were removed, she watched the ramp rise with her rifle aimed down it until there wasn't enough gap for any latecomers to fire through. Then she went to stand behind the pilot chairs while father and son got the launch thrusters started.

"Papa is opening the doors now," said Gerrit with a gesture to the roof above the shuttle. "So, all the men outside must be dead."

Oh, they're dead all right.

"Do I need to harness up?"

The boy passed the question on to his father. Stepka told her she'd be fine until acceleration toward Zuchola. That was good, she thought: good that the Polluxan hadn't forgotten the job they had to do before heading to the planet; good she could stand here and watch it. Good she wouldn't have to fit a harness over her bruising anytime soon.

Her toe oozed a tiny amount of blood. She noticed its hot line of pain as her adrenaline lagged. From Gerrit's bag, she retrieved small dressings and applied them to the digit as Stepka expertly lifted the shuttle through the bay doors. If he told her she'd need a crash couch for the burn toward the inner system, that would indicate this ship lacked inertial dampeners—and that would mean enduring high-G each time they accelerated. But the shuttle *did* have artificial gravity. It was lighter than standard, but strong enough to hold her in place as the shuttle separated from the cargo runner and moved further out from it.

The two Polluxans seemed pretty comfortable working their panels. They exchanged what sounded like routine questions, answers and observations.

Westermann came forward again. Spying a pasted strip of foreign words along the front of the helmboard, she pointed at them over Stepka's shoulder. The words seemed to use a mostly European alphabet with a few weird symbols tossed in.

"You understand that?"

"I don't reading this. But—"

"I can," said Gerrit.

Westermann blinked at the boy. "You can? Even the weird ones?"

He hummed and tapped his fingers on a datapanel.

More insistently, she asked, "*How* can you ...?" Her turn to wince as it occurred to her what he might have been through. "You've been around the Shinna a lot, huh?"

He glanced up at her with wide eyes, licking his lips nervously. "A few years. Papa *and* me. I understand a lot of their language."

"A lotta mine, too, kid."

"I'm pretty good on languages." He ventured a shy smile.

'On languages', she thought, and found her smile, patting his shoulder gently.

No sign of the carrier which had evidently moved deeper in-system on whatever its evil mission was. Once Stepka had moved the shuttle to a safe distance, he turned its nose around toward the cargo runner.

The freighter hadn't moved in response to their exit from it—adding credibility to the idea that no one was fixing its thrusters—but there'd been plenty of comms traffic coming out of it. The shuttle's comms panel had been lit up for the past three minutes with strident audio babble as the surviving pirates demanded an explanation. Westermann and the Polluxans ignored it by unspoken agreement. Only problem was they'd no doubt be sending comms to their carrier too.

Nothing I can do about that, she thought and touched the kid's shoulder again. "Our shields are up?"

"Yes."

"Ask your papa if he knows how to fire on that ship. Shoot it, I mean."

An exchange in their language, then Stepka rotated his chair toward her.

"I not shoot. Can't."

She peered past him at the freighter still spinning slowly in space and now a half-kilometer off their bow. Docked to the crew deck, her dog team's shattered skiff had a dark and ragged scar along one flank. Tiny flecks of debris trailed from inside. She wondered if one of those flecks was DeLuca. Or a part of its pilot. In the distance, off her starboard bow, a comet tail marked the vector of a huge and superheated chunk of *Artemis* moving away from them.

Westermann told Stepka, "Show me where the trigger is and I'll do it."

Once she'd traded places, the weapons control was easy to spot. A square video screen the size of her palm showed the zoomed-in image of the cargo ship marked with a crosshair. Below this was a simple orange button.

"How do I hit the drive when the damn thing's still spinning like that?"

"You wanting shooting *drive*? When, uh, da ship's ass come on da screen, you shoot it. You hit. Maybe you shoot five, ten, you hit drive okay."

Rolling her shoulders, she put her finger to the orange button. "Let's do this."

Laser fire jetted from beneath the shuttle's nose. The freighter's rear hull lit up momentarily before the tail shifted out of the sights. She released the button as lasers passed the ship by. A couple seconds later, as the tail rolled around toward the crosshairs again, she pressed the button. Stepka had been right: it took five hits before there was a small explosion. She leaned back in the chair. A bright blue flare announced the first detonation within the drive module. Explosions rippled along the freighter's body. Within seconds, the ship was unrecognizable.

"You mutts didn't wanna die, ya shouldn't't've come here killing *us*," said Westermann and gave the vaporized pirates a one-finger salute.

Immediately, she apologized to Gerrit for the crass gesture. His wide-eyed stare shifted from the ruined freighter to her and lingered on her face. Was that wonder in his gaze? Respect?

Vacating the chair, she told the boy's father, "No more bomb to ambush my people."

"We going planet now?"

She took one last glance toward the freighter where the bodies of her former comrades had also been vaporized. Then she moved toward the crash couches. "Yes, please, Mr Stepka. As fast as you can."

Chapter 6: Flight

*"You're all gonna die some day, recruits.
Just try not to be young when you do it."*

— Staff Sergeant Judah
Westermann's BASIC Training Instructor

ONCE THE INITIAL series of acceleration burns were
completed, Westermann wandered the cabin. In back, she
found cubbies haphazardly stocked with supplies: spare
clothing, anti-septic wipes, squeeze-bags of water, some
medicines and vacuum-sealed foods mostly bearing
labels from DCHC manufacturers. Had the pirates stolen
these last items? Looted them?

Traded, most likely, she thought with a glance toward
her Polluxan pilot.

After climbing and sneaking for an hour or more, and
after the scuffle with Moree, Westermann found herself

tired and sore, hungry and thirsty. She disinfected a water-bag before drinking her fill, and lay aside a half dozen of the food packs. Among the medical supplies, she found analgesic pills—whose foil packing she checked carefully for tampering before popping a couple. She found an instant icepack, which she activated and worked inside her undersuit against the tender side of her left breast. There was also a heparinoid gel that the faded label said was 'for the relief of contusions, hematoma, and inflamed veins near the surface of the skin.'

"If *contusions* means bruises," she told the label, "then I got contusions all right."

Once the icepack had done its work, she retreated to the shitter closet and applied the gel out of sight of her male companions. With her undersuit arranged properly again, she emerged, wiped her hands down with another antiseptic wipe, then gorged herself on three of the food packs while continuing to inspect the cubbies and the bulging storage nets fixed up near the cabin ceiling.

No e-suits were to be found. This was disconcerting given she was considering a prolonged visit to Zuchola. Biohazards or not, she reminded herself, a soldier being stealthy would be more flexible without one. And chances were pretty damn slim that she'd kick over the exact rock that released some new supervirus. After all, the scientists who worked down there did so without hazard gear—or so the briefings had informed her.

But no e-suit didn't mean she had to continue completely unprotected. One closet beside the shitter contained netting bags of personal armor pieces that could be worn either independently or buckled together.

Westermann pulled out a belly-protector. Because of the shuttle's near-standard artificial gravity, she was able to accurately weigh the piece in her hands.

"Not too heavy."

The thing felt tough as steel, but way lighter. It wasn't a composite she recognized.

All the pieces in the netting bags bore a faded brand logo on their inner sides, a CUSET-era name she knew from various military briefings on old-times stuff that scavvers valued highly: *Dupont Interplanetary*. Some pieces had plastic tags inside, but only one of these was still legible. It read, *98% TENSAR*. Another name she recognized. Tensar was a material the DCHC boffins knew well, but still couldn't reverse-engineer. Something about an organic compound they couldn't identify or replicate. The CUSET era had developed some crazy-good shit—hence the market demand for scavvers and smugglers. The stuff Westermann held still seemed in good shape, even nine hundred years after its manufacture.

"Old-times magic."

One glance down at her undersuit and she decided she'd be wearing some of this gear the next time she met pirates. A pair of boots seemed close enough to her size to be comfortable—although she didn't want to think how well-used they were. One of the Tensar thigh guards held a strapped-on side holster, so she slid a pirate pistol from its original holster and dropped it into this one, then put the whole piece aside. Stepka, she decided, could keep the other pistol; he had a kid to protect.

Lining up suitable pieces across the floor, Westermann

paused when she came to the net full of variously shaped chest-protectors. Some appeared to be designed with women in mind, and made her wish she'd had one when Moree hit her. Drawing a specimen out, she turned it over, inspecting it, then grunted.

"Looks like I got myself an armor bra."

Wearing the thing wouldn't be pleasant, but it would sure beat getting a bullet to the heart. Or another punch to the chest. The piece went on the floor with the others.

Stepka had come back to explore the food while she worked. The boy seemed content to stay forward, watching panels. As Stepka opened a food sachet and broke off a chunk of whatever it contained, she asked him, "How long? Until Zuchola?"

He poked the food into his mouth and mumbled a number which she instantly forgot, because her mind was elsewhere. All of a sudden, she was tired as hell, a wave of weariness making her sag against the storage nets.

Stepka offered the food package. "You some dis wanting?"

Thinking that his fingers had already poked around that bag, she replied, "All yours, guy."

"Gerrit," he called before rattling off a long sentence that included the word she recognized now for *bag.*

Sure enough, the boy scampered over to where his kit had been secured within the bulkhead netting between two side windows, fished out a clear plastic baggie filled with dried fruit then brought it over. It looked like apple. Westermann sniffed it carefully. Apple, all right. Her dad grew apples: eating apples, cooking apples, apples to feed the shentys. Westermann liked apple. A lot. She picked out a piece and started chomping on it, looking the scrawny boy up and down.

"The rest of that's yours, kid. But you could do worse than try some of the protein meals in there." Her head jerked toward the cubbies that his father had his head stuck in again.

Gerrit shrugged, retrieved some apple of his own, and returned to the helm.

So you don't wanna be big and strong then. Whatever fuels your fire, kid.

She followed him as far as the rearmost row of passenger seats and dropped into one. Over her shoulder, she asked Stepka, "How long to the planet again?"

"Seven hour," Stepka replied.

"Well," she yawned, "wake me in three."

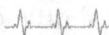

TWO HOURS LATER, Westermann was awake—without any help from Stepka.

After icing her bruises again, applying more gel and popping a couple more painkillers, she came forward to stand by the pilot chairs, exchanging a nod with the boy.

"Stepka, we got plenty of time to kill before planetfall. Wanna tell me all about the Shinna Caldones? And that big-ass carrier-gunboat of theirs?"

"I can some telling," the pilot shrugged.

The nap had only revived her a little and she retreated to the front row of crash couches. "You can *telling* me here. And Gerrit can translate both ways. That okay with you, kid?" she added, straightening her legs and stretching out to touch her toes.

"Yes. Okay." The boy swung his chair to face her and locked it in place.

Stepka also turned his chair to match his son's, and ruffled the boy's hair for a second.

"First up," Westermann said, "what's that big-ass ship's name?"

"*Dìon*," said the boy, without involving his father.

"*Dìon*. That mean something?"

He gave her a blank look. "Names don't mean anything."

"Um, they kinda do," she said, but didn't press the point.

Taking a moment to think up her next question, she watched the boy watch her. His attitude had definitely warmed to her since the shuttle capture and the destruction of the freighter. She hoped it was because he considered her a safe person, and not because he actually *liked* her killing bad guys. She didn't really know how kids thought, what was good with them, what was bad with them, what was normal, or what was … psychopathic or weird. Children were a mystery—despite the fact she'd apparently *been* one once. But she'd been Gerrit's age a decade ago, or more. She wasn't good with them, never felt comfortable around them. It wasn't exactly a core skill the Peacekeeper Corps looked for in their recruits.

Just treat him like a small grown-up.

"Gerrit, ask your dad where the Shinna Caldones come from."

The father prattled. The son translated. "Nearly two

hundred years ago, they found ships on Xerxes and got them working. That's what Haas told me. They left their Xerxes star system because it was full of other pirates. They had one ship—a *long* ship with one thousand people on it. And living animals, too. And the long ship was attacked at the Xerxes leappoint where it went."

"Attacked by the other pirates?"

"Yes. The long ship was hurt, but it got away from Xerxes system. They looked for another place to live. They went to Anticus system, but there was already pirates there. Clan Lobos and Blood Dogs."

"Yeah, we know about those clans being there. Cleaned them out a while back."

"I know about that. Big fights in space and on the planet with the Confederation. In 2970?"

"'80. And '81. And '82. No sign of 'Shinna Caldones' there. So where'd they end up?"

Gerrit didn't ask his father about this one. "Angelview."

"Angel ... view?"

"Yes. Angelview *Station*, I think it is named." He asked his father a question, then said, "Haas said it was a CUSET mining system. No planets. Just space stations and asteroid bases and *hasvoliken*. You didn't heard of it?"

She shook her head and thought, *Christ, this kid flips from great English to bad. Maybe he only learned some language in his games. Everything's got limits, I guess.*

"They made a good home there," Gerrit added for his father.

"I'm guessing you guys and me got different ideas of a 'good home.'"

Stepka was speaking again and Gerrit fell back into his role as translator, leaving out any contributions of his own. "What Haas told us was, the Shinna people came to Angelview and found a station to live in and a lot of big ships there, and lots of small ones. One was the 'big-ass' ship that killed *your* ship today. When the other pirate peoples came looking around, the Shinna could protect themselves with it. But they stayed away from you people."

Westermann's eyes narrowed at this last comment. "Ask your father exactly what he means by 'you people.'"

"Maoans, Centaurans, Caultans," Stepka answered via Gerrit. "The first three Confederation peoples. You're a ... Caultan, yes?"

"Caultan!" Westermann made a spitting sound. "I work for a living. I'm Centauran."

Gerrit didn't seem to see the problem, translating this in a carefree tone.

Stepka continued, explaining that Shinna Caldones didn't want to fight with *any* ships from other worlds because of the swift growth in power of the three main Confederation planets. Gerrit explained for his dad, "They saw what happened to the other pirates who fighted you. They hided in the shadows. Until *our* war. You know about the civil war? Between Castor and Pollux?"

"I went to school. I even passed that subject."

"Then you know that one of the pirate peoples helped Pollux. Starkillers." Stepka grimaced. With wide and fascinated eyes, his son watched him form his next words. Perhaps Gerrit had never heard his father speak of this before. "I'm not … um … proud of the war," the kid translated as Stepka found his voice again. "I was born after it stopped. When it finished, the other pirates ran away, but the Shinna Caldones came carefully into our system, the outer system. Castor didn't have leap-drives before the Starkillers came, they just build their power in the inner system and kept us under their …"

Here Gerrit mimed crushing something with a fist.

"Control," Westermann provided. "Domination. I learned about that, too. Then the Starkillers kicked the Castorans off Pollux and helped arm you guys, but that backfired and your planet fought both the Starkillers *and* Castorans."

"Mostly, yes. Until you people came. The Shinna came later, after the Confederation made peace, but the Confederation didn't keep enough ships in our system to see the Shinna being … stealthy out there."

"Yeah, it wasn't called the Confederation back then, but whatever. We were pretty dumb, huh, not finding the Shinnas out in the edges?"

"The Confederation ships were not so many and not so good back then, and the star system is big. And we have a lot of leappoints and they are hard to … um … guard. And Shinna Caldones sneaked around. They found some Polluxans who started flying out there, not many, but enough to work together on the *future*." It was Stepka's turn to pretend-spit as he chattered on. "My papa says *work together* is their words. They made some of us slaves like the Castorans wanted to. When Pollux joined the Confederation, we could fly free out of the system and some Polluxans could do scavenging and smuggling for the Shinna."

Westermann hummed a little. "Yeah. You got licenses for your own ships under emancipation laws, you got FTL, you got the chance to get real jobs offworld *and* explore the galaxy. I can see how that worked well for the Shinnas. Lotta people hate the fact we gave out licenses beefus-neefus like that. It's still goddamn impossible to track all the civilian vessels out there all the time."

He could only have understood a part of what she'd said, but Gerrit nodded anyway. Then he wriggled forward to the edge of his chair. "I need to piss."

Westermann suppressed a smile at the casual swearing. "Go ahead. Gimme that tablet of yours with the translation prog."

When the boy left, Westermann continued the conversation with Stepka via the tablet.

"That carrier they've got—the *Dìon*—and those little police-interceptors: they're old Chinese. Was this Angelview place a PRC site?"

"I told you it was CUSET. An industrial system."

She rubbed her eyes and yawned as she said, "Oh, yeah, you did. God, I'm tired. Anyway, so this PRC ship wandered around the void after PBT started killing colonies and ended up at Angelview. Their descendants were still there?"

"Haas asked them that once. They said the Chinese crew either killed each other or died of starvation. Same as the CUSET workers who'd been stuck in that system."

"No traces of PBT?"

"They didn't tell Haas anything about that. Or she didn't tell me."

"Angelview, huh? We could send ships there and capture the rest of these assholes. It's still the Shinnas' homebase, right?"

"I've never been there."

"But your kid has."

"My child?"

"You said Gerrit was a prisoner of the Shinna."

"Ah. Yes, but in my home system. Out at the edge of our astropause, the Shinna keep a small observation post. *That's* where Gerrit was."

She sat forward, remembering *astropause* from BASIC classes, something about the outer limit of a star's influence on the system around it. "That's gotta be, like, ten billion kilometers from Pollux."

"Further. It depends on the orbits, but it's a very long way, yes. And there were other children there, too." He added this with misery in his tone.

"Other...? *Godhack* it! These mutts!" She punched her thigh, then forced herself to calm. "You know, I'd really like to know how you got Gerrit back."

His eyes turned glassy. After a few seconds of this, she reached out and prodded him. He said, "I tinking about ... Sorry."

And then Gerrit was back, and it was too late to dig deeper into the grim details about what actions Stepka had taken at this observation post. But she considered the man with new respect. A man in a hard place, a man with no military training putting everything on the line to get his son back. And then he'd come here and the hard place had got even harder.

"That second handgun I kept," she said, leaning her head back toward the cubbies where she'd stowed it. "It's yours."

Stepka accepted this with a flick of the eyes aft, a glance toward his son, and a nod of gratitude.

Westermann closed the translation prog and hugged the tablet to her belly, relying once more on simple English and Gerrit as backup. "Where's the *Dìon* now? Any sign they know we're coming?"

Stepka ignored the first question and answered the second by jerking a thumb toward his helm panels. "Dey know. Dey sending comm to us for ten minutes."

"What?" Shooting to her feet, she came forward and saw a small screen flashing amber.

"Tightbeam, I think," said Gerrit as he leaned over it.

"And you're telling me this now?"

"I so scare to opening it," said Stepka.

"It's audio?"

"Ya."

"Recorded?"

"Ya."

"Play it."

The recording was brief and it was terse. Gerrit winced then explained, "They say why the *bad word* are you coming? What the *bad word* happen to the cargo ship? That's all."

"That's all. Jesus. Tell 'em... Tell 'em a Peacekeeper was alive and she killed some people, then she damaged the reactor. We had to get away before the ship blew up. But don't use your voice, yeah?"

Gerrit nodded, grinning. "I will text. I don't sound like them very much."

"No, you don't. Tell 'em the explosion's EMP blast affected some of our comms, so you can only text."

"I don't know some of those words in their language."

"Do your best. You know more of their language than me or your dad do, that's for shaz. Can you make 'em believe you're a Shinna?"

He thought about it. "If I use a *lot* of their bad words, and I be angry with them, they will believe it."

Gerrit typed his message, read it back to her—substituting "bad word" for all the cusses—and sent it with her approval. They waited in silence for an extended period before the reply came.

"Many more bad words," the boy explained, once he'd listened to it. "But they say, okay, then, you go to 'Red Star' and stay there. They call the planet Red Star," he added.

She caught herself reaching out to ruffle his hair the way his father had, pulled the hand back. "I know, kid. That's the old-times name for it. What else they say?"

"They are dropping a … a stomach ship at the planet. Maybe they mean a cargo ship. Some of their cargo ships carry a big container underneath them and it looks like a stomach. They can drop it and pick up new ones."

"Right, and what *else* they say?"

"They want us to help them and wait there."

"Wait for what?"

"For them to come back. After they finish."

"Finish what?"

He shrugged.

"The supply ship." She groaned. "They're chasing the supply ship. Well, it has a head start. Godspeed to 'em. Gerrit, you're doing great. They say anything else?"

"Just bad words." He glanced at his father, now up and pacing the deck and muttering to himself. "You want me to tell them to you?"

"Some other time, maybe. Do you know how many pirates will be on that cargo ship?"

"No, sorry."

"No bigs. I'm hoping not to engage them anyway." *For your sake, kid.* "One last question about their message. Did they say if anyone's going to the orbital station?"

"What is that?"

"Space station. This one's in geosynchronous orbit above the main planetside science base. I'd be surprised if the Shinnas didn't raid both at the same time."

He shook his head. "They didn't talk about it."

She got up, stowed the tablet, and started her own pacing around the cabin, doing something with her nervous energy. Both those research bases were filled with smart people—smart enough surely to get the hell out of there. Hopefully they were all on-world with somewhere just as smart to hide.

Dumping herself in a crash couch again, realizing she had to *save* her energy, she tried to imagine what it was like on Zuchola, having only ever seen a handful of vids and images about it. Down there, those scientists had two things going for them. They knew the terrain. And they had their own Peacekeeper stationed with them, someone to defend them before she got there.

If Tuccio even remembers how to fire a weapon, she thought with a humorless chuckle.

She'd met the crotchety Marine-lifer only once. And wished she hadn't. Tuccio had been stationed on-world for six tours now, and proved to be a bigger asshole than Badawi or Badillo. There were three rumors why he'd been stuck with this duty for so long …

One, he'd assaulted a senior officer and received this assignment as punishment.

Two, he had no family or friends to discuss any state secrets with.

Three, Tuccio was an anti-social *fernatz* with no life outside the Corps.

Westermann believed all three rumors were true.

Officially that single-person "garrison" on Zuchola was for protecting the researchers. More likely, its purpose was keeping an eye on them. The region they were in had no indigenous wildlife big and ugly enough to pose a threat. And no one had ever seriously expected an attack on this system. Three generations of captured pirates had consistently admitted a deep fear of this planet and its star system, after all.

Stepka still paced the cabin, muttering, while Gerrit stared at her.

She cleared her throat. "The orbital base has no defenses. Their defense was the *Artemis*—I'm sure your dad explained what happened to that? Yeah? Okay. The space station has an evacuation pod, big enough for all six personnel. They've probably used it by now. But I think the station should be our first stop."

"You want me to tell Papa?"

"Yeah. Tell him I need to check if anyone's still there. Then he can drop me on the planet and you guys can go to the emergency moon base. I'll help you find the coordinates when he's ready."

While father and son discussed it, Westermann returned to the lines of armor she'd arrayed on the deck and finished assembling a new combat outfit. Her nostrils flared at a trace of Stepka's B.O hanging in the air back here—then she caught a whiff of *herself*.

"Gonna smell a lot worse before this is over," she murmured. With a glance at the dressing on her toe, she added, "Probably gonna look it too."

Chapter 7: Approach

"PBT was the virus carried from the planet Zuchola/Red Star in the year 2145 to other settlements. It infected almost all other human settlements, devastating their populations and resulting in a collapse of civilization on all of them. Even, we suspect, Earth."

Iverson, Cohan & Kalili, *The Reunification of Human Civilization - a History of Recovery after the Second Dark Age*, Dogstar Press, 2998, page 4

FROM THEIR ANGLE OF APPROACH, Zuchola showed as a dull sphere, predominantly brown-green with tiny splotches of blue and white for water and clouds. By the time the assault shuttle neared orbit, its mothership had already departed the planet. Long-range scanners showed the giant vessel was millions of klicks away and accelerating as it tried for an intercept vector with the supply ship. Westermann had to presume the carrier had turned its own scanner on her, suspicious at the goings on out at the freighter.

As long as they stay away for the moment.

The supply ship was heading for the sun, or for a loop around it. No doubt they planned to keep enough distance from the carrier, hoping that the Shinnas would give up for fear of getting trapped in-system when *Valiant* arrived.

By the time the assault shuttle rounded the planet and the orbital station came into view, Westermann had strapped Shinna body armor over her insulated under-suit, slipped Shinna boots on over her bare feet and Shinna gloves onto her hands.

As she was stuffing Gerrit's satchel with water-bags, Stepka called to her, summoning her to the helm.

"This is bad, Peacekeeper."

Westermann studied the vidfeed he indicated. It showed the orbital at distance—and the damage done to it.

"*Very* bad," she agreed, vocal cords gritty from a few hours without conversation. She'd used that down time to eat, drink and nap. Down time, though, was over. "But not totally unexpected."

The Shinnas had hammered the drum-shaped space station into a ruin. The battered wreck leaked debris and ice crystals as it turned in a wild tumble. Laser-wounds gaped along its sides, its hull safety lights dark.

Westermann clenched and unclenched her fists. "Bastards haven't had time to get in there, steal things and get out again. What kind of pirates don't stop to loot before they torch a place?"

Pirates who are more interested in something on-world, she told herself, and once again was forced to hope their target wasn't something like PBT. *But what else could it be?*

She dredged up details from briefings she'd never thought would matter—and only half listened to. Red Star had three settlements back in the 22nd century. Two Chinese, one Corporate Union. Maybe the Shinnas want old-world crap, not the new stuff on the orbital. It wasn't a stretch to think they needed parts for the old tech they already had. Which would make their motives like those of scavvers the whole Confederation over.

Returning her attention to the subject at hand, she tapped her fingernails against the vidscreen. "Escape pod's missing, not blasted away. Looks like our boffins got out okay." She straightened. "You clear on where you're dropping me, Stepka?"

"I know where."

"How long till you set me down?"

"Twenty minutes."

"Like we agreed, then. You set me down fast—and you get the hell up to that moon, *faster*." Stowing her rifle for landing, she went to a crash couch to harness up. "And I know your captain was only pretending to be religious. But if you Polluxans *got* any religion, you might wanna pray that nothing goes wrong."

‑‑‑‑‑‑‑‑‑‑

IT WENT WRONG.

Atmospheric entry was tolerable. The shuttle was rated for it and coped fine.

But at nine kilometers from the surface, Stepka gave a cry of alarm. Before either he or Gerrit could explain it, something blocked the sunshine coming through the closest portside window to Westermann's seat.

She saw the dark, molded-wing profile of a Z-22 *Sparrowhawk* interceptor, its details clearer now as it kept pace with them, instead of speeding past like the one back at the freighter had. A good-looking craft. Good-looking like a wasp was good-looking. Caramel patches on gunmetal gray. Rows of running lights glowing bright even in full daylight. The muscular shapes of tactical laser emitters projecting from beneath each wing-arc. Knife-blade fins for stability in atmosphere, poking from the back like the twin dorsal fins of marine predators.

The craft had dropped in beside the shuttle as if in escort. And no doubt its pilot was using side-cameras to take a good look in through the forward windows.

Westermann's cussing joined the chorus of alarmed shouts coming from the pilot seats. There was other noise up there at the helm. Comms chatter. Urgent comms chatter. Demands for *something* in a foreign tongue.

The Z-22 vanished as the shuttle tilted sharply starboard. Ignoring the comms—ignoring *her* as she shouted at him—Stepka attempted to lose the smaller vessel via a series of braking and banking maneuvers that made the lumbering shuttle shake worse than when it first hit atmosphere.

When the *Sparrowhawk* pilot's yammering stopped, Westermann knew their danger had leveled up. Apparently, so did Stepka. The shuttle plunged into a nose-dive for a few seconds before the pilot somehow dragged it back, banked left, then leveled out. In those few seconds, Westermann had been aware of the ground rushing up at them, at the fact she could see topographical details now, mountains and ridges and splashes of vegetation. She'd also seen the twin lines of ion or laser fire passing over the shuttle.

Missed us once. Won't miss again. We're too big a target. Too big to dogfight.

But Stepka had not run out of ideas. Far from merely leveling out, the shuttle kept rising, angling sharply back toward space.

Okay. Damn good idea.

If they could make it to space again, the shuttle would have the advantage, using its heavy interplanetary thrusters to put serious distance between them and this—

A flash. A *whump* she felt in her chest. Debris sprayed past her, spearing forwards. Something tiny nicked her face; something larger struck the couch alongside her left shoulder. Air whistled and swirled around the cabin, pressure differentials causing a drumming in her ears. The laser strike had taken a chunk out of the back of the cabin, but blocked by the high back of her couch, she couldn't see how bad.

Bad enough.

Stepka screamed, his right arm flailing. Gerrit had his head over the boards, his hands working furiously. Past Stepka's left shoulder, Westermann made out a fist-shaped crack in the window. But from the way Stepka slapped his right hand over his left arm, it looked as if the hull fragment might have clipped him on the way through.

She touched a knuckle to a bright line of pain on her cheekbone. The glove came away bloody. Air currents were wild enough to open the cut up more. Not the worst of her problems. Beyond the forward windows, the ground rushed up at them again, sliding sideways as the shuttle rolled. Stepka's screaming turned to shouting. Commands for Gerrit.

"We're gonna crash," Westermann told herself. "We're gonna crash."

A curious calm came over her. A melting away of tension, of panic, of caring. There'd been so much struggle in her life: to break away from the farmlands of her youth, to find a survival job in Grace City, to pass her BASIC, to get noticed as a Peacekeeper. And today: just to stay alive.

But now, she felt nothing but a warm and cleansing acceptance of whatever would be. There was nothing she could do about her peril—the outcome was out of her hands. Perhaps many outcomes always had been.

Denise Westermann pressed her head back into her headrest, and hooked her boots around the struts that fixed the couch to the deck. She folded her arms over her armor. And closed her eyes.

DENISE IS TEN, a gangly girl with cropped hair and pajamas too short at the wrists and ankles. She's sitting on the edge of her bed. And she's fuming, the shenty-wool blanket clutched in her fists on her lap after the latest argument with her sister—

the ones that always turn into arguments with her mama who always takes her sister's side.

Denise's room is small, and while the homestead's outer walls are thick and sturdy, the plaster between her room and her sister's is thin. Enough that she can hear the quiet giggles and funny voices as her mother reads Heidi a bedtime story.

No bedtime story for Denise, though. Just an early night — which means more time to sit here stewing about the events of the day. The events of the week!

But then there's a heavy tread on the loose floorboard outside her door. Something in her chest let's go, relaxing.

Dad's home.

Where the hell has he been anyway? It's not like him to miss supper.

The shaggy, bearded head pokes in to offer her a sympathetic grimace. "Bad night?" *He asks it in Lebendspraaka, the only language he knows. Or chooses to know.*

"The worst," *she growls in reply.*

He slips in, closes the door softly at his back, mindful of the laughter and voices next door. They don't falter. He has one hand behind him, she sees. She looks a question at him, and he brings it around in front of him. It holds a nub of bone. Almost as long as his thumb. Shiny in the light of her lamp.

A skull.

The one she found? The one her mama tossed away?

"Is that...?"

Back against the door, he reaches over and places it on her nightstand, beneath her lamp. His face is sober now. "A reminder that life can be short. I don't know what you saw in it, but that's what I see."

119

She runs a fingertip over it. So smooth. He's varnished it. For her.

"It's a skull," she says simply. "It reminds me everyone had more inside than we get to see in everyday life. I guess."

He beams at her. "You're my clever kid, Denny. You always were. You'll go a long way in this life."

She's proud of his words, though she's not sure she really understands them. "As long as I never go a long way from you," she replies …

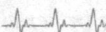

THE SHUTTLE STRUCK GROUND. Hard. Slammed her forwards into her harness. Careened across the ground, bouncing, shaking.

And Westermann thought, *I'm sorry I'll miss your birthday, Dad.*

Chapter 8: Planet

"Because of the planet's history, the first people to officially revisit the world in the 2960s (a crew of Chinese Maoan military) nicknamed it Zuchola (meaning "cursed"). This name stuck, becoming official during the 2970s."

Iverson, Cohan & Kalili, *"The Reunification of Human Civilization - a History of Recovery after the Second Dark Age"*, Dogstar Press, 2998, page 529

BUT THE SHIP didn't come apart.

It didn't explode.

And Westermann didn't die.

When the shuttle came to rest, she opened her eyes to confirm her status, to make sure. Aches and pains in her chest and shoulders from the harness straps. A resistance to taking a full breath because it squished her bruising against the inside of the armor bra.

Yep. Alive.

She let out a *huh* of surprise. Although she smelled faint electrical smoke, the shuttle remained in one piece. The arti-grav was off, leaving the floor with a permanent tilt to the right and toward the front of the ship.

For the next few moments, Westermann felt strangely divorced from all of this, like she was someone else sitting here waiting to be told what to do.

No. You gotta tell yourself what to do.

After unstrapping herself, she held on carefully to avoid falling or stumbling toward the helm. Gerrit was already out of his chair, butt braced against the control boards as he fussed with his father's harness. Through the cockpit windows, Westermann saw a dirty tan land-scape, lit by a star that was paler than Centauri's. A couple hundred meters ahead rose a cliff face, or the side of a hill maybe, blotchy with clusters of gray-brown vegetation.

"We nearly fell down there," Gerrit said.

Westermann had zero idea what he meant until she made her way to the back of his chair. The better view gave a better sense of what had happened ...

The shuttle rested with its nose poking over the lip of a shallow valley, or gully, what her dad would have called a *furchemvalde*. She assumed a river or stream ran through it, because the floor and lower slopes were thick with trees. She was looking down on the fluffy foliage forming their crowns, but the ones climbing the lower face of the opposite slope appeared to be three or four meters high.

"We'll go down there," she said, numbness and acqui-

escence evaporating, fresh urgency spiking. "That wood-
land provides cover."

Unless the Z-22 strafes it and sets it on fire.

She sighed, remembering *valdebrenden* running
rampant across the range of hills behind her childhood
home, and her father's exhaustion after fighting them for
many days straight to prevent their spread into neigh-
boring farms. As if summoned by her thoughts, a sharp-
edged shadow flashed diagonally across the valley.

We got bigger problems than wild fires.

She studied Stepka properly. He was white with pain
and muttering through clenched teeth as his son
unhooked both ends of a strap to form a makeshift sling.

"Your arm's broken?" Westermann couldn't check for
herself with the kid in the way.

"Break," Stepka confirmed.

"Bleeding?"

"No bleeding," Gerrit provided, getting the sling
around his father's back and shoulder as the pilot leaned
forwards. "But something hit him. That, I think." He
pointed his nose at a fat lump of metal lying loose under
the helm. Smaller pieces lay around it. One had
embedded in the back of Gerrit's chair like a dart.

She checked out the damage to the rear of the ship for
the first time. The ragged hole in the portside fuselage
near the toilet was the size of her head, and scorched
around the edges. Daylight shone through it, through the
spread of small windows along both sides, and through a
spread of thumb-sized holes in the starboard hull. There
was another hole closer to her position, a melt mark

where the laser had barely broken the skin of the ship. It had scorched the netting she'd stowed her rifle in. She didn't hold out much hope for the weapon.

But the people had made it. The three of them.

"Jesus," she gasped as a new thought occurred to her. She caught Stepka's eye, nodding in appreciation. "Good job landing with a broken arm."

"He helping me," the man replied. His good hand brushed his son's hair.

"He ...? Gerrit *flew*?"

"Ya."

"He *landed*?"

"Ya."

A flight simulator on a tablet was one thing. But this? *Clever kid.*

Gerrit caught her staring, and blushed with pride or embarrassment, or perhaps a little of both.

Damn clever kid.

Stepka's good arm pointed out the window and up toward the top of the valley's opposite face. "Scans voz saying dere's a small town. Dat way. Two hundred kilometer, maybe."

Long damned way.

"Forget the town." Navigating the cabin floor's odd angle, she climbed to where she'd stowed the rifle, listening to the tick of metal cooling, the thin whistle of breeze through the holes in the hull, the tortured buzz of something still running in the ship's thruster section. "Gerrit, help him to the emergency hatch."

As suspected, her rifle was a wreck, sliced in two by the *Sparrowhawk*'s laser strike.

"So much for that."

Fortunately, the shenty skull has dodged the destruction.

You're a lucky little bugger, ain't ya?

She unclipped it from the rifle and shoved it securely within the right side of her armor bra.

Okay, she thought, patting the holstered Shinna handgun she'd appropriated. *Next steps.*

The shuttle had made a belly landing, resting on top of its passenger ramp housing, so that exit was useless. She went across to the starboard emergency hatch and grappled with the lock-pin holding the release wheel in place. The damn thing did not budge immediately.

"Shoulda just gone to the moon, goddammit." She tried for a stronger grip.

Gerrit helped his father reach her side and balance against the bulkhead. "We go down to the trees?"

"If that interceptor up there doesn't torch us while we're stuck here." The pin shifted a little. Groaning, she put all her strength into it and pulled it free. Tossing it behind her, she pulled on the release wheel, growling, "I gotta work out more."

With a clunk, the hatch unlocked. The half-meter-thick chunk of hull swung outwards on its hinges, allowing Westermann to sample the dry and scentless air outside, to lean out and consider the surface of Zuchola.

"Hello, planet," she said, and eased herself out onto the dust and stones six meters from the edge of the gully. "All right, planet. You and me can be friends, right? You keep your viruses to yourself. And I'll … think of some way to pay you back."

With her help, Stepka slid down to join her. With his balance back, she nudged him toward the gully's edge.

Her eyes were on the sky while helping Gerrit out, squinting against the hazy glare. "I can't hear that interceptor. Can you?"

"No."

"Not sure whether that's good or bad." The sky was sheeted in thin cloud, the sun glare painfully bright through it. She dropped her gaze, blinked a few times, saw a dust haze the far side of the gully. "I got a bad feeling they've landed. C'mon."

The Polluxans made a diagonal descent of the gully wall with her bringing up the rear. She touched the shenty skull with the tip of a gloved finger.

"I'll make it out," she told her dad so many lightyears away. "I'll make it home. I may be late, but I'll make it. Promise."

The soil was firm but rocky, allowing good purchase. This side of the line of trees below them, grasses grew to ankle-height, to hip-height. Some clumps bore a flower that looked like a crème-porcelain tulip.

Gerrit had his bag over one shoulder. Father and son entered the shade a few meters ahead of her.

And a hot thread whistled by. A bullet. Dirt kicked up to her right.

Dropping with her left hip and shoulder angled uphill, Westermann pulled her pirate sidearm while scanning for the shooter.

There!

The Z-22 pilot. Wearing a full flight suit with its helmet visor down. On one knee and attempting to steady his aim with a handgun of his own. Unbalanced and hurried, he was having trouble. One hundred meters away across the gully, the distance didn't make it easier for him. Two-handed, Westermann fired her own pistol, getting a feel for the kick. It was ballistic, and it was a big bastard. By the third shot, she had it under control—and had the pilot scrambling for cover behind a rock.

Movement above her. She snapped her head that way. Another damn pilot. Same flight suit and helmet get-up. Jogging along the top of the gully for a better position, this guy carried a laser rifle. Vaguely, she remembered Jeng saying that Z-22 *Sparrowhawks* held two crew, pilot and tactical officer, so maybe the *Sparrowhawk* had dropped this guy over this side before finding a secure spot for a vertical landing on the other. Either that was true, she thought as she rolled onto her belly and got the gun in position, or more than one interceptor had landed out here.

Westermann fired up the gully once, twice. Dropped the guy. Couldn't believe that she had. Couldn't believe how steady her aim had been. Didn't hang around to overthink, or give him time to cry out, or let his buddy draw a bead on her. Got to her feet and made a crazy run directly down the slope to the closest trees.

One more bullet sliced through foliage from above her, showering her in fluffy leaf-things. And then she was sure the pilot had lost her—she was out of his sight. She slammed bodily into a tree near the bottom of the gully, forearms up to absorb as much of the blow as she could, spun around and pitched sideways into the dirt, lost the pistol as she rolled over rocks and claylike soil before bumping up against another tree trunk. She waited a second for the pain to kick in. Nothing. Nothing *new*, anyway. The armor pieces had protected her from the rocks she'd tumbled over.

Several meters further downhill, a flat creek bed. Dry. A gully devoid of animal or insectoid noise. Faintly, a man's cry carried down from above, the pilot asking after his comrade. There came no reply.

Where the hell were Stepka and Gerrit?

She scrambled for the pistol, wrapped a hand around the grip, came up in a crouch.

Someone gave a low whistle.

"Over here, my darling." A woman's voice.

Westermann swept the weapon's business end across the slope to her left, seeing nothing but the spongy trunks of the gully's crazy fluff-trees, and pockets of dirt, and a pitted boulder, and tufts of dry pseudo-grass.

"Don't shoot me, darling. I like living as much as you do."

"Where are you? *Who* are you?"

"A researcher, dear. And we're in here."

A hand appeared from the jumble of vegetation where two trees had come loose from the soil and toppled together. A tanned hand. Holding a rag. Or handkerchief.

Weapon up, Westermann advanced on it. When she was close enough to make out two faces through the screen of twigs and branches, she lowered the gun. One of the faces belonged to Gerrit. The other, a woman her dad's age.

"It's a nature hide," the woman said quickly. The hand

twisted to point around the far side of the jumble. "You climb in under the exposed roots there."

Shouts rolled down the valley. More pirates arriving to help the first two search.

God, I hope there's room in there, thought Westermann and scrambled around the side.

Chapter 9: Allie

"During the CUSET era, "PRC" was the non-Chinese label for the People's Republic of China, an Earth nation/country and an economilitary superpower. The PRC led much of the early space exploration of the mid-21st century, but were later surpassed by the alliance of corporations that became known as the Corporate Union, or CUSET.

The PRC remained a powerful player in both terrestrial and extraterrestrial affairs until the onset of PBT. Because the Confederation has, to date, no contact with Earth, it is unknown whether this nation/faction still exists within the Sol star system.

The PRC's official language was Mandarin Chinese."

Iverson, Cohan & Kalili, *The Reunification of Human Civilization - a History of Recovery after the Second Dark Age*, Dogstar Press, 2998, page 34

A HOLLOW HAD BEEN dug into the hillside behind the

fallen trees, and lined with soft plastic walls to keep the dirt out. Scanty light filtered through the screen of enmeshed trees covering the hide, but the researcher had a single work light dimmed and set atop a bunk in the back. As Westermann's eyes adjusted, she saw the space was plenty big enough for its four current occupants—and wondered how long their rescuer spent in here at any one time. It smelled clean. As did the woman herself. At least, if she was giving off any body odor, it didn't stand a chance against hers and that of the Polluxans.

Shelves and a low work desk lined one wall of the makeshift cave. A white box under the bunk was probably food storage, a fridge. No toilet-bucket, Westermann noticed, grateful for small mercies. Set against the screen of branches, a clear water drum with a filtration system indicated the researcher had her own system for capturing whatever moisture was to be had in this arid landscape. Two drinking bottles stood near the water drum's tap, both full. The weather outside had been hot and dry, and the gully windless, making Westermann glad for the insulation of her undersuit. By contrast, the air within the hide was cooler against her face and tasted of earth.

No one spoke as the minutes ticked by. Early on, Westermann heard muffled shouts from outside and the crack of sporadic ballistic gunfire which must have been intended to scare them out of hiding. None of it seemed nearby, and after a while there was nothing to hear except for her own breathing and an occasional pained hiss or grunt from Stepka who'd retreated to the bunk at the back of the hide, sitting on the floor against it.

With immediate danger passing, Westermann studied their rescuer. The woman could be anywhere between fifty standard years and seventy. Her eyes were round, appearing brown in the low light. Dark freckles dusted both cheeks, and some of these vanished inside deep wrinkles. Her brown hair was streaked with gray and tied out of the way on top of her head.

When they hadn't heard any exterior noise for forty-five minutes, Westermann made ready to crawl out for a recon. The researcher placed a hand on her arm, surprising her with its bony strength.

Warm breath brushed the wound on Westermann's cheek as the woman murmured, "I'll go, darling heart. I know the place better. And I'm skinnier and more flexible." To underscore the point, she patted the armor on Westermann's back.

Westermann nodded. It had been hard squeezing through the opening wearing this. And the lady sure seemed tough enough.

When she'd left, Westermann sniffed at one of the water bottles, then drank deeply from it. By the time she'd screwed the lid back on, Gerrit was drinking from one out of his bag. He passed it to his father.

"All right?" Westermann asked them.

Gerrit said, "Yes."

Stepka merely grunted. He gulped from his son's bottle.

The researcher returned inside of twenty minutes. Lifting a thatch of vegetation, she ushered Westermann out into the hot air in the shade of the fluffy trees. Unconcerned about the volume of her voice, she said, "Two went that way along the gully. Two headed west. All wearing full environment suits, so either they hate our local sun, or they're worried about PBT."

"If they're who *he* says they are—" Westermann pointed back at the hide, meaning Stepka. "—they've never walked in open air or under a sun."

"Most pirates haven't," the researcher shrugged. "Anyway, the searchers are a fair way off now. They must think you went back toward KnowTown. That's our main research facility."

Westermann knew that, but didn't comment, too busy moving down and onto the creek, out of the shade, studying the trees and the slopes, listening for interceptors. The cut across her cheek prickled as UV rays bore into it.

God, this sun!

When she'd been a girl, her school had dragged her along to a camp on the edge of Centauri's largest desert. Some dumbass teacher's idea of getting kids interested in ecoscience. The worst thing about that camp had been the heat. Zucholan heat wasn't as bad, but it sure came close, the sun stinging the exposed skin on her cheeks now, the bridge of her nose. The dry air sucked the moisture from her nostrils and mouth.

Once the Polluxans were out of the hide, the researcher joined Westermann at the creek and asked, "Your name. His? And his? You're a Private? Okay, then. Officially, I'm Doctor Alcantara, but everyone calls me Allie."

"Not a nice way to meet, Doc. Allie, I mean."

"No. But I'm glad to see you. And since you three

survived that ship crash up there *and* crashed right above me, it seems like luck's been on your side."

Thinking about the safe haven on one of the moons up there, Westermann said, "If luck was on our side, we wouldn't have crashed the shuttle. We wouldn't be here at all."

Allie accepted this with a shrug and waved the Polluxans over. "When you were flying—or crashing— did any of you notice the range of hills seven kilometers that way?" She pointed along the creek in the opposite direction to where the search party had gone. "No? Well, you were busy at the time. They're the foothills of the Araga Massif. We have a bunker there. Two hours' walk, if we're being careful. Maybe a little more with his injury. My comms suddenly cut off when these ... visitors arrived. But that hill bunker is probably where my colleagues went once they'd been warned away from KnowTown. It's a bigger shelter than this, and better supplied."

Westermann pointed the direction Allie had. "That way?"

"We'll follow the creek the first half of the hike. Takes us on a slightly circuitous route, but it will provide cover from those hunting us."

"Copy that," Westermann said.

Allie made them wait while she delved inside her hollow for her water bottles and satchel.

Westermann took the opportunity to study the mess of vegetation over the hide. When Allie emerged, she asked her, "What were you *doing* out here?"

"My job." Allie's gaze shifted to Westermann's

holstered sidearm. "And you can do yours by escorting us to safe haven."

"That's the plan, ma'am. How long's this gully?"

"From here? About a kilometer, before the terrain around it slopes lower to meet it. When it's flowing, the creek drops into a narrower arroyo. We'll follow that for a time. Eventually, we'll have to get out on the open plain, but we'll have long grass as cover because the soil is more fertile over that way." She raised her eyebrows. "Shall we leave?"

"Damn right, we shall."

DOCTOR ALCANTARA—"ALLIE"—SHOWED zero anxiety as she took short, confident strides behind the Polluxans. Westermann stayed close to her, watching the horizons, watching the skies. While the males shuffled and stumbled along, finding their ground-legs, the researcher moved with fluid grace. She was straight-backed, brimming with nuggety strength. Her skin had the look of quality, aged leather. Exposure to this region's fierce summer sky had darkened it deeper perhaps than it had naturally been.

"You're part of the leappoint interdiction team?" she said suddenly, turning her brown eyes Westermann's way.

"The dog team, yeah."

"You're a long way from the Exclusion Zone."

"Tell me about it."

Sympathy softened the older woman's features as she

studied Westermann's various scrapes—the ones she could see, at least. Her gaze lingered on the scuffed non-regulation body armor. "Rough time?"

"My team had it rougher." Westermann glanced at the position of the sun. "But yeah, it's been a long and shitty day."

"A long and shitty *morning*," Allie corrected her with a sympathetic crinkling of her face. "Afternoon by your shiptime. Late morning on this part of the planet, I'm afraid. Your long day's got longer to go yet."

Westermann took a moment to curse the sky and the local time.

And herself.

I got us shot down. Why didn't I just get us to the moon base? We'd be safe up there.

Performing a slow turn to check their six, she asked, "The bunker we're headed for: how come *you* didn't go there already?"

"Didn't have three newcomers to care for, did I? Besides, I prefer it out here. In the wild."

"What, with dust in your nostrils, and your throat all dry, and the sun burning you?"

"And the quiet. The interesting work. The pure, untainted ecosystem. But that's not all of it." She heaved a sigh. "The real reason is I didn't want to get cooped up in the station with Harkin, if everyone was heading there. She's another scientist. A real *tulalâ*. About as much fun to be around as your counterpart, Corporal Tuccio. You know Tuccio, I presume?"

Westermann grimaced. "Met him once. And that was enough. I totally get you."

They walked a dozen meters in silence before Allie said, "Tuccio always calls your inspection team a 'dog team.' Just like you did. Is that an idiom?"

"Not an insult, ma'am."

"Idiom isn't insult," the woman said. "It means slang."

"Oh. Right. Well, it's an idiom, then. Boarding team members are called dogs because we go in, sniff around, dig crap up—and bite if someone threatens us."

"Colorful."

"Yeah," said Westermann, picturing the dead bodies of Jeng and Badillo and Badawi, even though it was the last thing she wanted to think about. "We're colorful."

Fifteen minutes later, they scampered across open ground between the gully's end and the place where the streambed dropped into a dusty arroyo as Allie had promised. Inside the shallow gorge, the males took the lead again, Stepka with his pistol in hand. Westermann let them because she could keep an eye on them without turning all the time. Once more, the women fell into step beside each other.

Christ, thought Westermann, *is this really happening? Am I walking around on Zuchola?* She withdrew the tiny skull from within her armor, rolled it around one palm, rubbed a thumb over the beak-hook and ridges and smooth spots, feeling anchored once again by its presence, its reality, summoning the peace it had brought her that moment her dad placed it by her bed.

Allie asked, "Is that from an animal you hunted, trapped ...?"

"Found." Westermann pressed the cool knob of bone to her cheek for a moment.

"Found? Where?"

"Our farm. When I was a kid. Thing had been dead a while and the local sheet worms had already picked its head clean. It's a ... My parents raised these animals called shentys. Lots of 'em on Centauri. Cute little buggers. Only grow knee high, but real profitable if you farm 'em right."

"I know of them. I'm not much of a meat eater, but theirs was palatable when I tried it."

Westermann wondered if the word *palatable* was Spanish. Where did Allie come from, anyway? Her accent was hard to get a fix on. "It's not bad," she said. "High protein, low fat. But I got sick of it as a kid. And we mainly kept them for wool."

"I'm glad you didn't kill the animal yourself." Allie tugged at the scarf she'd been wearing around her throat and pulled it up over her hair. "Can't abide people who hunt and trap animals for trophies."

"This ain't a trophy." Westermann put it away, against her left breast this time; though it pressed against the bruising, it was also close to her heart. And the pain might keep her keen, keep her alert.

"Not a trophy." Allie studied her. "I can see that now."

They trudged onwards with the sun burning off the thin cloud layer as it rose higher to reveal a pale blue sky. Every breath of wind that rustled the thickening grasses along the lip of the arroyo had Westermann flinching and angling her handgun. At one point, she was sure she heard the deep hum-whine of an aircraft in the distance. Nothing came of it. It could have been imagination. She winced when the toe she'd cut in the freighter pinged with pain. The dressing was slipping off it. But this was a bad place to remove a boot and fix it. As swollen as her feet were starting to feel, she didn't think she'd get it back on again.

"These two were *captives* of those pirates?" Allie asked her.

"The kid told you that?"

"Muttered something like it when he came into the hide ahead of you."

"Well, *he* was. Stepka kinda worked for 'em."

"Oh."

"It's complicated. He got the kid away from them and hid him on his cargo runner. But then the Shinnas forced him ..." Westermann passed a hand across her face. "You know what? They can tell their own stories over drinks at your bunker. Speaking of which ..."

A waggle of her hand and Allie passed her a water bottle from her satchel. They each took a swallow before the scientist put it away.

Allie said, "They're lucky to have you."

Westermann puffed out her cheeks for a second. "No. They're lucky I haven't got 'em killed yet."

"What do you mean, dear?"

Hearing the weariness in her own voice, Westermann explained, "They should have got a real soldier. *You* should have. If I'd made Badillo listen to me, he'd be here looking after you guys. Or if Badawi hadn't ..."

If I hadn't taken my eyes off Haas, Badawi would still be here.

If I'd made Stepka go to the moon base, him and his kid'd be safe now.

A hand on her shoulder plate stopped the flow of thought, tugging her back to the here and now.

Allie eyed her fiercely. "A real soldier? That's what you said? We should have gotten a real one?"

An unwelcome lump had formed in Westermann's throat. She nodded, lips pressed together, teeth grit.

"Private Westermann," the researcher said, "you made it this far alive, didn't you? You got those two here alive—whoever the hell they are."

Westermann made a dismissive sound, and gently broke the scientist's grip on her shoulder armor. She swallowed to melt the lump in her throat. "I got this far by hiding. I got here by ambushing a bunch of Shinnas on their shuttle when they weren't expecting it. I got here by Stepka and the kid flying me here."

"And you exchanged gunfire with the pirates hunting you, allowing these boys to hide with me. All of this sounds to me as if you've done *exactly* what needed to be done. At every point. And you're doing it now. Right now."

Westermann swiped sweat from her brow and looked away. "But—"

"I'm no expert, my darling, but it seems to me that the actions you've taken *are* soldiering. And you've done it well." Allie straightened and offered a theatrical salute, smiling.

Despite her situation and despite her weariness, Westermann returned the smile. "If you knew anything about soldiering, Doc, you'd know ya don't salute Privates."

"My mistake," Allie chuckled.

Westermann started walking again, keen to keep close to the Polluxans. "You know, I been thinking. And you're a smart person, so maybe you can help me with this. I really don't get why they didn't garrison *more* soldiers here. More on the planet, I mean."

"You don't need to be scientist-smart to figure that one out," the researcher said as she trailed after her. "The reason is money. It's always money. Governments have plenty of competing demands for it, good and bad. But they always *always* spend it poorly. For example, there were originally three ships in the blockade, up until eight years back, which is when the key tappers decided one ship was plenty. Unfortunately, egalitarian civilizations like ours are run by bureaucrats and money-counters, not by people with common sense and foresight. The *tulalâs* in the Confederation government won't spend more in this system than the bare minimum."

Westermann flashed her a wry look. "You think they'll change their minds now?"

"They will, darling. All governments everywhere spend the money on the problem *after* the crisis has passed."

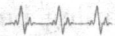

AT ALLIE'S INSTRUCTION, they eventually climbed out of the arroyo onto an expanse of grassland and into the embrace of a freshening wind. Westermann felt the welcome touch of moisture in it. Clouds piled up far to the southwest, spreading across the horizon. Low hills curved around that horizon in a smudge of brown; the darker, higher smudge of mountains rose behind them. From here, the hills appeared slashed by titanic claws, the darker lines were ravines, the shadowed pockmarks hollows.

Here and there, the landscape sprouted a pair or trio of more substantial plants. Allie pointed to a copse of familiar billowy trees poking above the grass. "We rest over there. Then it's about three kilometers to the hills."

"More than halfway there," Westermann reassured Gerrit when the boy looked back.

He accepted this with a serious nod and pushed on. The kid seemed to have more energy than she did at this stage.

God, he should be a Peacekeeper.

They made the trees in under five minutes. Westermann sent Gerrit to keep watch from the far end of the copse, and checked on Stepka's makeshift sling.

Sinking to her haunches, Allie nursed her satchel on her knees and fished out a data device. "Our visitors didn't torch the meteorological satellite. How kind of them. That's a storm coming in from the south-west, dears, but it looks as if it'll miss us here. We can rest here for ten minutes or more, if you want."

"Ten is plenty," Westermann replied.

Allie regarded Stepka skeptically.

Westermann pointed to the belt that Gerrit had earlier commandeered from the nature hide and tightened around his father's upper arm to hold the bone in place. "He's doing okay. And he'll make it to the hills. Won't you?"

Stepka nodded. "I making it. I making Gerrit safe."

Westermann raised her head when a tree shook because the kid was climbing for a better position. "I think he's doing a pretty good job without either of us."

"He is smart boy," Stepka agreed, eyes shining with something other than pain.

The trees shook again, this time from a hard gust of wind. To Allie, Westermann said, "Storms get rough round here?"

"This time of year, they're frequent, but tame. The word 'storm' is probably misleading. More like heavy showers." She faced south-west. "That'll turn into a rain dump for an hour or so, then there'll be blue skies again."

"You get *frequent* rain? But this is dry country." Apart from the weird-ass trees currently shading them, the area reminded Westermann strongly of the Nuevo Chihuahuan region on Centauri, a hot savannah no one had bothered populating even in the CUSET era.

Allie put her data device in the bag, laid the bag on the ground and stretched out beside it. "Well, it's technically a steppe, so it's really about evapotranspiration or how long the water hangs around before it runs off or evaporates. Regular rain here keeps the grasses healthy, but in most places there's not enough water hanging about for trees to get a foothold. Except in areas like this where it pools against bedrock beneath the topsoil." When Westermann stifled a yawn, the researcher let out a self-deprecating laugh and patted the Peacekeeper's boot. "All right, I'll stop lecturing."

"Sorry. Tired."

"I can imagine. Sit, dear. There's water in my bag. Drink."

"I'm fine," said Westermann sitting beside her, but not reaching for the water. She tilted her face toward the canopy above, a natural awning that seemed as brittle and insubstantial as sea foam. Despite this delicate appearance, it was withstanding the assaults from the gusting wind just fine, losing only the occasional tuft of ... whatever that was. Flowers? Spores?

Following her gaze, the scientist said, "Okay. I'm going to lecture some more. Can't help myself. They're interesting trees, yes? And this is an interesting region on an interesting world. There's a common misconception that there's not much life on Zuchola. Because this world is *old*. Older than your homeworld. Older than mine. Older than Theseus. Older than Earth. And people see that it's a little bare." She rubbed her hands in the gritty soil. "It's worn down. But, as these trees demonstrate, there *is* life here. What you can't see is how *much* life! Most species are simply too smart to run around in the open near us weird-smelling humans. And before PBT, humans weren't here long enough to find and catalogue many of them. Besides, those settlers were too preoccupied bending the planet to their will and fighting over it to get to know it."

Westermann considered her a moment. "You love this place, don't you?"

"If I didn't, living here would be hell: it's not like I get to leave very often. But yes, darling, I do love it." She lifted some soil and let it slip through her fingers, allowing herself a soft sigh.

"What did you mean, settlers bending it to their will?"

Sitting up, the scientist dusted her hands. "They were trying to change it to suit them. Like colonizers did wherever they went, throughout our species' history. In the few short years of settlement here, the list of environmental vandalism was long and familiar—and spectacular for such modest immigration levels. Planting rice paddies where native marsh grasses already thrived. Destroying a cave system for the minerals beneath it. That kind of thing. Given the potential shock on this ecosystem from the arrival of humans, you might almost think PBT was a punishment, a judgment." Her eyes twinkled with dark humor.

"Oh, God," moaned Westermann. "Don't tell me you're a Millennialist." There were many sects among Millennialism. One of them preached and favored aloneness, living in nature. Another called *any* environmental disaster 'the Godhead's wrath.'

Allie laughed. "I'm far from being one of those damned fools, my dear, I assure you. I was merely waxing philosophical for a moment." She shifted into a more comfortable position, crossing her ankles. "This planet has a morbid name when you translate it from the Mandarin—one we scientists are happy to keep if it discourages popular interest in the place. And we keep quiet about what a beautiful world this really is."

Westermann could grudgingly agree that these trees had a *kind* of beauty. But the rest of the bland countryside she'd seen? Not so much.

Reading her thoughts from her face, Allie said, "The

beauty is in its wonders. Its creatures! They are my life and my heart."

"Like what?" So far, Westermann hadn't seen so much as a bug or fly.

"Like the racers." She bared her forearm and slapped it with the other palm. "Animals as long as this, with hind legs as long as their bodies. In the mating season, their males array themselves across hills and ridges, posturing, waiting, fanning out their colorful neck frills to attract attention. Meantime, the females pace out a course in the land below: one hundred meters, one-twenty. Then ... they *race*! For the affection of the male. And the right to have their eggs fertilized. Also ..." She looked around her a moment then pointed. "You see those marks in the dirt there? What we call scurry tracks. From a form of *Vermis pampinus*."

"Vermis ...?"

"A worm with tendrils. Probably a thousand of the little buggers in the dirt beneath us right now."

Westermann got to her feet smartly. It wasn't the idea of worms. She was a farmgirl. Creepy crawlies had been a part of life. But *Zucholan* worms?

Allie grinned up at her and continued, "Pampinus reproduces by growing offshoots of itself which act for a time as limbs before reconfiguring their own cells and breaking off as a kind of clone."

"That's ... hinky."

"It's magnificent. And don't get me started on the ecosystem in these trees. Beetloids. Bark parasites ..."

Stepka had been watching the conversation with growing alarm, demonstrating again that the lub-head understood English plenty fine when the mood suited him. At this last comment, he called out, "Gerrit! G'uiit de bome! G'uiit de bome!"

Reluctantly, Gerrit started climbing down.

Grinning, Allie asked, "So, I shouldn't mention the vossoko tigers up in the mountains?"

"No, you shouldn't," said Westermann. "And it's time to go."

The older woman pouted. "That wasn't ten minutes."

Westermann offered a tired smile. "The biology lesson made it feel longer."

She helped Stepka up. The grim and sun-reddened pilot looked to Allie for direction, and Allie pointed.

"Okay, thank you, *mavrow*." Stepka followed her instruction, gathering his son as he went.

The two women followed, stepping out into sunlight so harsh that Westermann found herself wishing for the clouds to hurry up and get over here to block it.

"Mavrow," she said, mimicking Stepka. "G'uiit de bome. God, I wish everyone would speak English or Spanish like they're meant to."

"But that's another problem with any form of colonialism, darling. Even a benign and well-intentioned one like our Confederation. Where's the fun in everyone speaking only one or two languages? Where's the color?"

"Well, I speak three."

Allie patted her arm as if awarding a young student a consolation prize.

"What the hell's *mavrow*, anyway?"

"In Taal, their language, it means *madam* or *dear lady*."

"It does? Huh. He never called *me* that." Westermann

tugged at her braided hair and made herself turn a full circle to watch their backs. Then, thinking of diverse Confederation cultures, she gave the scientist a lingering sideways look, assessing her again. The woman's accent was an interesting one. A fusion. A little Caultan, a little Centauran, a little Maoan even. But there was another flavor in there. And she'd used that word a couple of times. What was it? *Tulalâ*?

"Ma'am. Allie. You mind me asking where you're from. Your accent ..."

"I was wondering when you'd ask. Everybody does. My dear," she said, "I'm Xerxian."

Chapter 10: Pirate Treasure

"Since initial contact was made with the highest-developed Xerxian planetary nations, these three factions have maintained a kind of stalemate when it comes to negotiations.

Each displays a tension between preparedness to formalize a deal with the DCHC in the future and retaining diplomatic and cultural uniqueness and independence. Only one of them has introduced formal Confederation English and Spanish classes as part of early childhood education (and as part of some career training). This, at least, shows a welcome long-sightedness.

Perhaps, in a decade from now, the various Xerxian pirate factions will also respond positively toward Confederation attempts at peaceful contact ..."

From *"The Case for Welcoming Xerxes as a Member-World"*, (Report No. WT-RD 36.4 for the DCHC Joint Committee on Member States, tabled January 2997)

"YOU'RE *WHAT?*"

She'd barked it loud enough to prompt looks of alarm from Stepka and Gerrit. She'd also frozen in place, gaping at the researcher.

Allie put her hands on her narrow hips, turning to her. "Oh, relax, darling. We're not all pirates, you know."

"But—"

"Most planet-Xerxes folks are ordinary people, just humans. Not the barbarians you think we are."

"How did you …? What are you … ?"

"Doing here? My *world* might not be a Confederation member, but *I'm* a Confederation citizen." Allie motioned impatiently with one hand and when Westermann fell in step with her again, she continued, "I left Xerxes twenty-eight standard years ago. That was the year the joint Maoan-Caultan battle group appeared in our system, knocked out a pirate fleet in the outer regions, then came planetside to say hi. You know of this?"

Westermann shook her head. "Never heard of it."

"Hm. No one ever tells me what is and isn't classified. Perhaps you shouldn't mention I told you. Anyway, they spent ten standard months meeting with delegations from three Xerxian planetary nations. Mine was one of them. My leaders rushed me into an interpreter position, since I'd been studying old CUSET data since my childhood. Long story short, I started an affair with one of the diplomatic staff. Begged for asylum and the chance to serve the greater human race. I got it, too. I was whisked off Xerxes. And placed here. Where I've lived ever since. Where I couldn't do any harm, couldn't send any secrets back to Xerxes, and couldn't ever return."

"They think you're a spy? Still?"

"Well, you didn't look so friendly a moment ago when you learned of my origins, did you?"

"I … Sorry."

Allie waved it off. "Even on my furloughs every three years, I'm only allowed to travel to Pride of Mao. And I'm watched the whole time. They call my escort a security team. But the security's for the DCHC and not for me. Anyway, my original point about diversity and color within the Confederation still stands. Stepka's language, Taal, is a minority one, but as interesting as any other. And just as valid."

"You speak a lotta languages? Even though you don't travel?"

"As I say, I began my Confederation career as an interpreter. I love languages. And I get books and streamies and recordings sent to me here. You're … Centauran, right? West Centauran by your accent. Which means you speak one of those dialects. You said three languages. What's the other one you speak, besides English, obviously?"

"Spanish. Teeny bit of Mandarin, too."

"I speak a *lot* of Mandarin." A gap-toothed grin and a mock-humble dip of her head. "I spoke four Xerxian languages before I left there. And my hobby—you *have* to a have hobby living here, dear, trust me—my hobby is French."

"What the hell's 'French?'"

The woman rattled off a string of nasal, musical phrases, then said in English, "That's French."

"Oh."

"A dead language. But beautiful. And oh my God, reading science in French is like reading poetry."

"I'll take your word for it." Westermann turned three-sixty degrees again, watching behind, watching the skies. The talk of West Centauri had brought her a pang of despair.

Dad.

Tramping through rib-high grass, headed for a base that might be tough to secure, she felt a trillion years away from the end of this thing.

No, she told herself and checked the time again. *Not a trillion years. Two or three days till* Valiant *makes it to the planet. All you gotta do is stay in the bunker and wait it out like Gerrit was doing in his shipping container.*

Once *Valiant* arrived, there'd be a further two or three days of debrief. There'd be a preliminary inquiry. She'd be late seeing her dad, but they'd tack extra days onto her leave, either to reward her, or to sideline her—depending on whether they decided her actions here were good or bad.

Were they bad?

I took my eyes off Haas. I let her get a weapon.

But I was kinda distracted by the hackin' big pirate carrier attacking our launch ship.

Ah, crap. Let the inquiry decide.

Thunder rolled from the south. The clouds pushed closer, spreading. But as Allie had predicted, it didn't look like they'd quite reach this area.

The scientist said, "You have a plan for our safety, Private? Once we're in the bunker?"

"Well, if the pirates don't know about it—"

"It's tucked between two hills. Hard to see. No maps for it at KnowTown because it's a contingency for something like this."

"—then Corporal Tuccio's the one to set the plans. He outranks me. All you'll have to do is hide out with him for a couple more days and you'll be safe."

"'You'll be safe?' As in, the boy and his father and me?"

"Yeah."

"And where will you be?"

"You said something about me being a soldier. Once you're safe with Tuccio, my job's not hiding out. I gotta find out what these mutts are up to."

"The pirates? What if Tuccio already found out?"

"Tuccio? Hilarious."

"So, what? *You'll* stop them?" Allie lowered her voice and paused a moment, her hand hooking on Westermann's forearm bracer as they walked, coming in close. "I'm not doubting you. I don't know you, Private Westermann; I don't even know your first name. I don't have any right to take an interest in your wellbeing. But a young woman like you? I wouldn't like to see you throw your life away on pointless heroics."

"I'm not thinking of heroics."

"Finding out what the 'mutts' are up to?"

"Doesn't mean I'm gonna engage them. And whatever I do, it ain't pointless."

"All right. All right. It's up to you, my dear. Unless Tuccio forbids you leaving the station. Come on. Quicker we get there, quicker you can be gone again." She picked up speed, closing the distance to the Polluxans. "May I share another secret with you, Private Westermann? Besides the one about the diplomatic meeting on Xerxes thirty years ago. Given that you want information on the pirates, dear one, I think you'll enjoy this: I know why they're here."

Westermann squinted at her. "*You* do?"

"I think so. The first thing you need to understand is that the Shinnas are not pirates."

"Wait. What?"

"Stepka called them Shinna Caldones earlier. The language I heard among the searchers would confirm that identity. Shinna Caldones are a nation. On Xerxes. Have been for well over four hundred years."

"*What?*"

"They inhabit the Riesco Peninsula on our planet's largest continent. And some islands off its coast."

"Stepka said these chubs have been hanging out in some other star system."

Allie pursed her lips. "He's probably correct about *these* 'chubs.' If I can explain systematically ..."

"Sure," Westermann deadpanned. Why couldn't this woman bottom-line anything? Still, she had to admit that any intel was useful intel.

"A common misbelief that persists among Confederation military is that the asteroid factions were the only Xerxians to regain spaceflight. Not so. For the first forty years that the initial two asteroid-civ clans got their intra-system ships operational, they commenced raids on our planet. That ended when two planetary factions recovered spaceflight also. Both reverse-engineered it because the pirates let three of their ships be shot down over land. The Sevens Party captured two and Shinna Caldones got the other."

"The Sevens Party are a nation?"

"They *ruled* a nation. Still do, I'm told. There was a leap forward in technological and industrial progress. The Sevens set weapons platforms in orbit to resist further incursion which put an end to the raids by outer system clans. Meanwhile, Shinna Caldones got to exploring our moons along with the space between us and the closest planet."

"I never heard any of this."

Allie made a shrug with her face. "Definitely classified, this time. Even if it wasn't, it's not the kind of history to filter down into your high schools. Not the kind of history your military puts a lot of faith in, either. Which doesn't make it untrue."

"I bet the Shinnas just loved the 'Sevens' having weapons platforms overhead."

A small laugh. "Oh, indeed. As did other nations around the world. It was certainly *the* thing that tipped the balance of power on the planet toward the Sevens. Today, they are the most powerful nation on Xerxes. They reached out recently to recommence dialogue with the Confederation, by the way. I bet no one told you that, either."

"How do *you* know about it?" The woman had mentioned an affair back in the day; was it still going on?

"The Ministry of Trade, Treaty and Diplomatic Affairs

consulted me, that's how. Then decided not to take me along. Well, no matter. This is home, now."

Westermann found herself reluctantly interested in the history lesson. Mostly because of Allie's promise to solve the mystery of the Shinnas. But also because there was secret knowledge here, stuff she wasn't cleared to know. "So, the balance of power shifted toward the Sevens?"

"Yes. And when they first put those platforms up, the other nations aligned for an eight-year war against them that, well, let's say it *diminished* their power for a couple of generations."

"This was, like, two hundred years ago?"

"Close enough. The war also gave the Shinnas, as you call them, the chance to venture further from our home-world without Sevens molestation. When they finally captured a Luján Clan FTL-shuttle in 2840, they gained a working leapdrive. *That* enabled the building of a huge exploration ship which they launched in 2851. It was never heard from again. Not on Xerxes, anyway."

"Stepka and Gerrit said they left Xerxes system in a 'long ship.' They reckon it ended up in a system called Angelview."

Allie frowned. "That's the Shinna name for it?"

"CUSET name, I think."

"Never heard of it."

"Me neither."

Allie sighed. "So much data still lost since the old times. There could be a hundred settleable systems out there we no longer know about. There might be ones the original superpowers kept off the records to hide them from each other."

"It's a big galaxy," Westermann agreed. "So, what Xerxian nation were you? You don't look like a Shinna."

"Nope," Allie laughed and pinched the skin on the back on one hand. "I'm assuming you've seen some of them outside their e-suits? My complexion's a tad better suited to this environment."

Feeling the sun-kissed tightening of the skin on her brow and cheeks, Westermann had to agree. Her pale skin had been locked up under artificial light for months.

"I come from the Sevens' nation."

"Shit," Westermann complained. "This is a lot to get my head around."

They began skirting a dip in the landscape, a bowl from which grew more of the fluffy trees. A few hundred meters past it, Westermann could see that rocks poked above the grass. The closest of the hills was not much further beyond that, a humpbacked projection rising from the otherwise flat landscape they'd been trekking across.

"Angelview," Allie murmured. "The Shinna might have been breeding there for one hundred fifty years. Might be hundreds of thousands of them now."

Westermann shook her head. "Don't think it's that many. Stepka didn't think there was a planet there, so there's not much room. Just space stations. Mining crap. And a couple old Chinese ships."

Allie's eyebrows waggled and she hummed to herself.

"What?"

"Chinese ships?" she asked. "You're sure?"

"So he said. The ships they brought here are Chinese, apparently."

"Then, my darling, my suspicion about why they're here is more likely to be accurate."

"This," said Westermann, "is where I really need you to *spit it out*."

The researcher took a moment to respond, concentrating on picking her footing carefully across the increasingly uneven surface between tufts of grass. "Because they have some old Chinese ships already, it means they've had access to old Chinese files. It means they've found out about a *fleet* of Chinese ships left here in this system." They were coming around the side of the bowl now and Allie pointed to the hills ahead, speaking to the Polluxans. "Not much further, boys."

"*What* fleet of ships?" There'd been nothing about that in any of Westermann's briefings. Unless—maybe she'd slept through that part.

"Back in the early, messy months of settling this system in the mid-22nd century when they were squabbling over it with CUSET, the PRC snuck a reserve fleet here—a secret one we think, because no Confederation data miners have found any record of it in Corporate Union files. We stumbled over the fleet about twenty years back. One missile cruiser, two big long-range interceptors like your interdictor, and one non-FTL gunboat."

"Goddamn. They hid 'em here?"

"Mm-hm. Anchored them to the dark side of a barren rock close to the star. We presume that was in case CUSET decided to challenge Chinese custodianship of the system." She was quiet a moment, scratching her chin. Then: "There's a lot of mystery about that, still. This fleet was so secret, so dark, that when the virus erupted on the

Red Star colonies, those four ships didn't lift a finger to help. They let their settlers appeal to CUSET for CUSET help."

Westermann scratched her nose. "Well, duh. No mystery there. They were wasting their enemy's resources on a dangerous virus outbreak while they kept their distance and their health."

Allie gave a mild smile in return. "That's not *exactly* what happened, Private. PBT spread quickly enough among Chinese colony worlds and habitats. But your point has *some* merit."

From somewhere east of them came the deep whine of a familiar aircraft.

"Down!" Westermann barked.

The four dropped into crouches among the tall grass, scanning the skies. The Z-22 sounded a fair way off and Westermann couldn't locate it. Eventually the noise faded and she got them to their feet again, urging fresh speed.

Allie continued, "My suspicion is this. This Shinna faction is here because they want to go home. To Xerxes. But they've probably been scared of returning through the Xerxian leappoint until now—all they remember is the gauntlet they had to run when they left through it."

Westermann gave her head a little shake: the woman was chatting away as if nothing had just happened, as if they weren't in danger at all.

"If their aim is to return to their ancestors' world after generations of exile," said Allie, "they know they need some serious protection. Even a modest fleet of old-world battleships is rather formidable ... by Xerxian standards, at least. Also, let's be real here: they know enough about the Confederation military to be scared of your capability, but not enough to realize you're not a threat unless they shoot first."

"Which the idiots did today."

"Sadly. From the sounds of it, they also had an idea how poor your blockade really was and brought enough firepower to win that fight convincingly and quickly."

Westermann made a face. "Probably found out about the *Artemis* by jacking data from another captured Navy vessel. We've lost a couple in the last thirty years. And ..." She rubbed her forehead. "I'd forgotten about this. Two years back—before my time—an unidentified ship leaped into the Exclusion Zone, then leaped out eight seconds later."

"Yes. Yes, I remember that, too. And no one knew who it was, but it looked like an old-times survey ship."

"Right. *Artemis* crewers reckoned it had its exit nav preset. So, it was only here for the time it took some hack-head to tap *go* into the helm."

"And *go*, they did. But a survey vessel can take a lot of scans and imaging in eight seconds."

"But eight seconds wasn't long enough for *Artemis* to wake up, let alone get close enough to target lock 'em. No one knows if the ship was even manned or not. Damn. These bastards have been planning this a while."

"So it would appear."

"Okay. *Okay*. So, there's a bunch of Shinnas at your KnowTown base, looting the place or whatever. The carrier dumped 'em here, then went off to grab the secret fleet, *not* to chase our supply ship. But, Jesus, they'll have to work fast if they wanna get four ancient ships operational enough to leap out before *Valiant* gets here." She broke off when Allie began chuckling softly. "What now?"

"There is no secret fleet. Not anymore. The Shinna carrier is off on a ... a ... damn, what's that classical phrase? Wild duck hunt? Something like that."

"*We* took those ships?"

"DCHC Navy did, yes. Eighteen years ago, they cut them up for parts, and hauled their remains out of here."

"Cut 'em up? They were in bad shape?"

"Very. The anti-meteorite guns on their hiding place failed centuries ago. And there's plenty of space rubble in the inner system. I'm told it only took a few collisions for the ships to be ruined. One interceptor was 'pulp,' a spacer told me. As was the small habitat within the asteroid."

Westermann scanned the skies again with a palm shielding her eyes. No sign of the Z-22. If the hunting party had given up looking for her, that was just fine with her. She said, "The carrier's off on its wild whatever hunt. But why'd it drop a crew down here? What's on Zuchola for them? And please don't say PBT virus."

Allie snorted. "There's no thousand-year-old super-virus to be found around here, dear. Ground zero for PBT was on the far side of the planet, for one thing. For another, the thing burned itself out centuries ago. I'm afraid most of the fears around that disease are really just superstition. Or, to be fairer, based on misinformation. Which suits the DCHC and us researchers just fine. There's nothing on this planet to interest anyone but scientists, darling heart. No, the Shinnas roaming around here are only here for three rather plain and ordinary things: intel, loot … and fun."

"Fun?"

"Murder and mayhem."

Westermann kicked a thick clump of grass, wishing it was a Shinna's head. "And the bastards are hacking good at that."

Chapter 11: Bunker

"We don't pay you to be nice, Recruit Westermann.
We don't pay you to think.
We pay you to keep the peace for our democracy and its citizens.
Anyone or anything that's threatening that peace ain't there for
you to play nice with, or get into dialogue with, or get into deep
thought about.
They're there for you to neutralize."

- Staff Sergeant Judah

WESTERMANN STUMBLED as her boot rolled off a wayward rock. Losing her footing, she fell heavily on one kneepad, swearing when the impact jarred her aches and pains. Gerrit reversed direction toward her, offering her a hand. She softened her eyes at him and waved him away.

"You are okay?" the boy asked her, hovering.

"Yeah, I'm good." On her feet now, Westermann performed a brief shuffling jig. "See?"

When he nodded and scampered back to his father, she quit the ridiculous antics and grimaced, bending to adjust the kneepad that her fall had skewed sideways. "At least, I'm not dead yet."

"Private Westermann," said Allie, "if you insist on chasing pirates all over Zuchola, then you may be soon."

"I told you—"

"Where will you go to gather your intel, anyway?"

Setting off again, Westermann forced the older woman to give a little jog to catch her up. "I was thinking of KnowTown."

"Which is one hundred eighty kilometers away," Allie said and pointed back the way they'd come.

"Your guys made it out here. I'll make it back there."

"You won't."

"Watch me."

"What I mean is, by the time you've walked there—"

"There's no cars at the staff bunker?"

Allie shook her head. "My colleagues used an underground fast-rail to get to the refuge. Then they destroyed the KnowTown end remotely."

Westermann squinted at her. "You're lying."

"Not a nice thing to say to someone you just met."

"You're lying. To be nice to me."

"I'm not. And there aren't any cars or bikes or flyers in the bunker."

"Seriously? That's stupid."

"That's bureaucracy. I told you about the key tappers and their obstinate lack of foresight. The Navy and the

Parliament have gotten cheap and lazy when it comes to Zuchola, my darling. No one really thought a day like this would come. So: no vehicles at the bunker. The cars and bikes have been utilized elsewhere. I didn't have one, even way out here, as you may have noticed." Allie pointed at her own boots.

"Surely Tuccio thought ..."

"Tuccio's biggest concern every day is choosing the cereal or the eggs for breakfast."

"Hack this."

"When we get to the bunker, dear, you're going to recuperate. You're going to sit this out with the rest of us, and let *Valiant* storm in and handle it. If there's anything to handle by then."

"You mean let a bunch of hackass pirates get away with their loot. Get away with mass murder."

"If you let yourself survive this, then I'm sure you'll get to go kill pirates at some stage in the future."

The half-mocking comment was a kind of final straw for Westermann. She let out a roar of frustration that had been building, and building. Stepka and Gerrit startled. She scooped up another loose rock and flung it as far as she could. "These hack-lovin' bastards came all this way, put all their money on arming 'emselves with Zuchola ships, and there's nothing here for 'em. Nothing. Which means they killed *all these people* for nothing!"

Alli's face twisted wryly. "That's what bad people do, dear. Insane and desperate people."

It was true. Westermann couldn't argue with that, and had no reply. All she could do now was complete this escort duty, then help Tuccio defend the refuge bunker if necessary. And treat the various scrapes and bruises she'd accumulated.

Westermann was just another dog soldier. A nobody. The bigger picture was beyond her reach—and beyond her abilities.

She hated that.

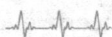

WITH FATIGUE SETTING in and impotence dragging at her heart, Westermann stopped pushing the group, allowing the final kilometer's walk to become a slow trudge. Her reasons for urgency had gone. There was nothing more to be done about the Shinnas. And because she saw and heard no more Z-22s, she figured they'd given up the search for her group.

The four entered the narrow gully between two sparsely wooded hills. Allie had indicated this as the path to the refuge bunker entrance. Despite the fact that Westermann wasn't sheep-dogging them, Gerrit maintained his pace well out in front. His father, by contrast, dragged his feet, keeping close to the women now. He clutched his wounded arm tight to his body, his shirt drenched in sweat. When one of the pilot's boots caught a stone, causing him to stumble into Westermann, it forced her to dance sideways to regain her balance. As she did so, Gerrit shouted and broke into a run of his own.

"Wait!" Allie called after him, but the boy vanished around a turn in the ravine. "Young rascal. He's sighted the entry."

The news should have been reason for relief, for relaxing. They'd made it. They were here. But it was unnerving to have the kid out of sight. The three adults found a new reserve of strength with Westermann pulling ahead of the others.

She turned the bend in time to see a hinged door swing and click shut. The door had been set in a kind of pillbox halfway up the hill to her left. Perhaps it was placed up there to prevent rain runoff seeping through it and into the facility. She began climbing the slope—until Allie stopped her with a gasp of alarm. The researcher put a finger to her lips and pointed to the summit of the hill, through the smattering of pillow trees. The hill appeared to level out at the top. And the tips of a Z-22's forward-curving wing poked out over the edge. Westermann swore and dropped into a crouch, head swinging to survey the ravine and its myriad hiding places, ears straining.

Climbing after her, Allie stared up at the interceptor wing and stage-whispered, "Unlikely my colleagues captured that thing."

"Bastards are in there. So's Gerrit." She caught Allie's gaze. "Take Stepka. Find somewhere to hide."

A moment's hesitation, then Allie replied, "Very well."

Allie turned her head to watch the pilot make it two meters up the hill before slipping down on his good shoulder, grumbling in Taal. It was obvious he hadn't noticed the interceptor above them.

The researcher added, "He's in rough shape, but I'll get him back to my nature hide. It's safe. And you know where it is."

"We'll catch up."

Allie started away but Westermann grabbed her arm the same way the older woman had grabbed hers during their walk.

"Be safe."

Allie patted the Peacekeeper's hand. "You, too, my dear."

And then she was sliding on butt and heels downhill. At the bottom, she started a hushed argument with Stepka while they hurried away.

After completing her climb, the Peacekeeper paused at the bunker entrance, her pistol aimed skywards with the sun-warmed frame against her cheek. She lay her other palm on the door handle, taking slow breaths.

"Well, Denny," she told herself in a gruff imitation of her father's voice. "You wanted to be a soldier."

Westermann slipped one finger insider her armor bra to shift the shenty skull to a more comfortable position. The finger lingered on it in a kind of wordless prayer.

Then she opened the door and plunged into the gloom beyond.

Chapter 12: Gerrit

"It's not your job to enjoy this training, recruits.
It's not even your job to pass this training.
It's your job to embrace *it.*
When your life is under threat, you're gonna need instincts you can trust."

- DCHC Peacekeeper Marine Corps proverb.

A STAIRCASE.

It plunged thirty meters into the earth at a sixty-degree angle, lit only from the corridor lights at the base. Westermann paused, her eyes acclimatizing—and found herself staring at a corpse a quarter-way up the steps.

Corporal Tuccio. Face down with his Peacekeeper fatigues blackened and bloodied.

Blood pooled beneath him, dripping down another riser to form a smaller pool beside his leg. Someone had trod in it, leaving a trail of right-boot prints for a meter down to the lowest step where it faded.

Taking the risers carefully, she paused long enough to confirm his status, though the confirmation was hardly necessary. Westermann was officially last Marine standing.

The pirates had shot out the stairway globe here; glass crunched underfoot as she passed the body. She pressed to the wall to avoid it, kept moving down.

No door or hatch at the base: the staircase and corridor were joined. The passage stretched ahead for fifty or sixty meters, illuminated by soft yellow globes at ten-meter intervals. Walls were bare plasterboard, not even painted, discolored with age. No closets fixed to them. No switches she could see. Openings along the left-hand wall indicated a half dozen rooms, no actual doors, doorframes only, as far as she could see from here. A close door faced her from the far end of the corridor—a washroom? A dark opening beside that suggested another staircase.

As Westermann's senses adjusted to the new location's acoustics and recycled air, she noticed the smells. The dull tang of old construction materials. A newer, fainter hint of sour body odor—not hers, male, definitely. The sharp bite of gun smoke from ballistic weapons, like the one she carried. And there was sound. The soft clatter of items on benchtops, a closet door banging closed. A burble of conversation—hard to pinpoint its distance from here. Beneath it, the trace of someone whimpering—she thought this might be coming from a different room, a closer room. And snoring. Yes: snoring. Possibly from inside the nearest doorway.

Keeping as light on her feet as the boots would allow, Westermann peeked into the first room.

Occupied.

The snorer. A bearded pirate stretched across the lower of two bunks against the back wall. On his back, with his hands folded over his stomach. A transparent bottle stood on the floor in line with his head, half-full with a clear liquid. His suit helmet sat beside the bottle. One of his hands was speckled with blood. More of it spattered the front of a leg, coated the sole of his right boot. On the mattress by his pillow lay an identical pistol to Westermann's. His grimy, shabby e-suit was unarmored, same as all those worn by the cargo runner boarders.

He wasn't alone in the room, either. A woman scientist had been cuffed to the foot of his bunk, forced to hunker against the bed because of the shortness of the chain. A young woman. Westermann's age. Blood had dried on a deep cut across her nose and another below her swelling left eye. Apart from the facial wounds, she didn't appear to be harmed anywhere else. No disarray to her clothing. Still had her boots on.

Small mercies, I guess, Westermann thought and put a finger to her lips.

Her good eye widening, the scientist hunkered down even more, attempting to shrink.

Moving to the pirate's side, Westermann took a pillow from the top bunk, used one arm to fold it in half against her body then caught the ends in her free hand. In one fluid movement, she clamped it over the pirate's face, pushed her weapon against it and squeezed the trigger. The man didn't get the chance even to unfold his hands. She released the pillow and left it there to soak red.

The dead man's pistol went into her holster, a spare.

After unclipping a small set of handcuff keys from his suit, she released the prisoner. "Anyone else captured?"

The woman shook her head, wincing as the movement made the pain flare in her face. In a hoarse whisper, she said, "Took them in the kitchen and ki … They're dead."

"They're still there?"

"Y-yes. I think."

"The pirates, not your friends. Are the pirates all in there?"

"I … Not sure."

"You been in here a while, in this room?"

"Fifteen minutes. He …" She peeked up over the bed, recoiled and turned away. "He chained me and went to sleep. Insane. A … minute ago … I think … maybe two or three … A kid came through the entry. Ahead of you. Or a woman? They fell down the stairs and I heard them crying at the bottom while someone ran to … to get them. He—" She glanced at the bed then away. "He slept right through it." Her face said she could scarcely believe that he'd done that, that any of this had happened.

"He the one who hurt you?"

The scientist dabbed fingertips to her facial wounds. "Him. And a woman."

"Then we got nothing to regret about them dyin', you copy me?"

"Okay."

174

"How many pirates?"

"Six. Including him."

"You're sure?"

"Yes."

"So, five, then. Where's the kitchen?"

"Second to last doorway. Second-last doorway."

"The other rooms are …?"

"Bunkrooms. Three more. Then the kitchen. Then the storeroom. Then the door at the far end is the comfort station. Kitchen's big."

"Good detail. Gimme more."

"About the kitchen? Uh. It goes back a long way. Four long tables in the middle. Couch on the side, this side …" She indicated the lefthand side as someone would face into it. "Bookcase past the couch—someone could hide behind it if they wanted."

"You're doin' good. Now. You know where Doctor Allie's wildlife hide is? About seven klicks from here? Yeah? Great. Know the way? Even better. You go there. Now. Fast. And you stay in that hole until relief arrives. If I don't find you, someone from *Valiant* will."

Some change in the refuge's sounds or ambience snapped her attention to the corridor, put her senses on red alert. The sudden slap of shoes on floor got louder; Westermann dropped into a crouch with her weapon up. A man pelted past the doorway, with only a glance inside. A man with one arm held tight to his chest. The weapon drooped in Westermann's hand.

Stepka.

Their eyes had met for only a quarter-second, but it

had been enough to see the madness in his, the desperation. He was here for his kid, unable to leave it to her.

Westermann took a fistful of the scientist's shirt and dragged her into an upright position. "Go. Now."

A shove sent the woman running at the doorway. Westermann stepped through it a second after the scientist, placing herself between the woman and harm's way, trying to hiss a coherent warning to Stepka. But the pilot wasn't responding. And things were spiraling too fast for her to intervene. He took a cursory look in the next room as he passed it. A second later, he skidded to a halt then backpedaled to it, framing himself perfectly in the doorway while Westermann tried to wave him back, his pistol coming around but shaking in his hand.

Shouts erupted from the room. Stepka got off the first shot, but the recoil from the large ballistic handgun pushed his aim up and exposed his torso. He took several bullets and one laser strike from whoever was in that room. Shuddering under the blows, he staggered backwards and against the corridor wall, sliding down, weapon falling free.

Westermann snarled, pulled the second pistol from the holster, strode toward the doorway with both muzzles centered on it. The shouting continued from within.

A male Shinna with a laser pistol ventured out to consider Stepka's body when he should have checked the corridor. Westermann blew a chunk out of his scalp. From a doorway toward the far end of the corridor, another male Shinna appeared. Dual-wielding, she fired three shots that missed but sent him ducking back inside the room that must have been the kitchen.

Two weapons had been used on Steak. She still had one hostile in the room closest to her she needed to—

Ballistic rounds punched through the wall beside her. One struck her armor under her left arm and over her ribs. The hammer blow spun her around to face the direction they'd come from, to face the fresh holes in the plasterboard between her and the hostile. Spying movement through the holes, she returned suppressive fire, then rushed the doorway to squeeze off another couple of rounds. The woman inside was already on her back, gargling blood that dribbled out and along her cheeks. She wore similar armor to Westermann's, but one bullet had torn through her shoulder between the plates while another had punched into her upper chest below her throat where the chest pieces didn't cover. She gagged and spasmed, but her limbs didn't move. Her open eyes paid no attention to Westermann.

Curled up on the top bunk with his knees to his chest, Gerrit regarded her with fearful eyes. He had a bruise on his right cheek and a cut on that ear, but seemed otherwise intact.

"Shit," Westermann gasped. "*Shit!*"

I coulda shot him.

She ordered him to stay, then braced in the doorframe to check the corridor again. The remaining pirates were still in the kitchen, thumping around. Making barricades, maybe—or battering a hole into the next room. At the end of the corridor beside the comfort station, that was definitely another staircase. She didn't think anyone could have made it from the kitchen to either of those in the time she'd been distracted here.

She checked the loads on both handguns, put one of them back in the holster, stooped and snatched up the laser emitter dropped by the dead bastard in the hallway. There were people to check on now: the scientist had made it out safely, but Stepka was dead as a stone. A large-caliber bullet had hit him in the heart or close to it. And the smell of charred offal indicated the laser emitter had burned into a lung.

A red haze descended over the corridor, that same red haze she'd experienced catching the shuttle pirates watching *Artemis*'s destruction as entertainment.

That same cold strength flooded her limbs.

She met Gerrit's eye where the kid cowered on the bunk. "Do. Not. Move."

Then she clamped the laser emitter carefully between her teeth before grabbing an empty trash can from the corner. Along the corridor she stalked, her handgun trained ahead, keeping her tread light while her breathing whistled in her nose. When she made it close to the kitchen door without incident, she heard mutterings and whisperings, the rasp of limbs against firm objects and surfaces, enough to give impressions of position and distance within the room.

Taking a step into the middle of the corridor, Westermann tossed the trash can at the wall a few meters behind her and plucked the laser from her mouth with her left hand. As the trash can struck and pirates started firing through the wall there, she charged the doorway with her right index finger repeat-squeezing the handgun's trigger, left index finger clamped down on the emitter to squirt a continuous line of red destruction around the room as she kept moving on a lateral trajectory, hoping to dodge return fire.

Flames licked up along furniture from the laser. Pieces blew out of the turned-over tables the Shinna had sheltered behind. When her right shoulder hit the side wall, she realized the ballistic weapon was dry and the laser was slicing into three bodies already prone behind the tables. She released the depressor, checked behind the bookcase the scientist had mentioned, and turned back to the downed hostiles. Two of the three wore the flight suits she'd seen hunting her near Allie's hide. More bodies lay piled against the deep room's back wall: science staffers. Westermann didn't study their wounds too closely, but kicked the Shinna bodies hard. No response.

Every single one of the pirates down here, it occurred to her now, had taken their e-suit helmets off.

Relaxing.

Havin' a good time.

Bastards.

A quick check of the comfort station proved it was empty. She returned to the kitchen. The laser's charge was near-exhausted. She tossed it, checking over the other pirate weapons in the room. One guy had the same model handgun as hers; she prodded his suit pouches until she found his spare mag, counted eleven rounds through its side window, dropped the empty one out of her gun and jammed this one in. Then took a second to touch her shenty skull inside her chest armor though she wasn't sure why.

The kick in her side from the pirate bullet pulsed in time with her heartbeat.

Shoulda brought that damn gel off the shuttle.

Shoulda brought the icepack.

For a moment, she considered raiding the fridges for one. But there was more important shit to do. Including getting a kid to some kind of safety.

Someone had lined up one-liter bottles along a kitchen counter. One spouted water from a hole made by a ricochet. With the long Shinna pistol still in one hand, she used the other hand to grab two bottles by their necks, then marched from the room. Returning to Gerrit, she lay them beside him and dragged over his satchel. The bag's contents had been dumped on the floor. His tab with its flight simulator game lay cracked and warped from being stomped on.

"Six dead hostiles," she told him. "No more pirates here. Okay? They're done, gone."

He swallowed and gave a little nod.

She had other news to give him, now the fight was done, now the red mist was fading. But she didn't know how to say it, not yet. Instead, she kept it practical: "Put the bottles in the bag, but stay here. I'll be back in a moment."

He threw out a hand. "Don't ..."

"I'm coming back, Gerrit. Promise."

Back into the corridor.

By coincidence, Stepka's hooded eyes stared directly at the dead pirate between him and the bunkroom door, as if accusing him.

"You poor, idiot bastard," Westermann whispered. He'd gotten caught up in something bad, for sure, and he'd done it out of financial need, probably. He'd still known it was hinky, right from the beginning. But the thing she would always respect about him was how hard he'd tried to get his son out of it.

That wouldn't be consolation to Gerrit. Not yet. Not for a real long time.

She wondered, should she move Stepka's body? Take him to the bedroom where she'd found the scientist, lie him there with a blanket over his face? Should she lie to the boy about this, until he was back in the nature hide? She really didn't know how kids thought.

If this was my dad lying here, I don't know what I'd do. But, she realized, *I'd wanna know about it. I'd wanna face it.*

"God," she said to herself. "This ain't a job for a dumb soldier."

She went to the first bunkroom anyway, tore a sheet from the top bunk and brought it back to spread over Stepka's torso up to his chin. His head, at least, remained uninjured. She closed his eyelids and thought that he looked peaceful. Kind of. A rosette of blood seeped through the sheet.

"I shouldn't did run in here," Gerrit called to her suddenly, his Conglish faltering.

She winced. *I wish the same, kid.* She didn't say that, though. She had to say something different, something that'd prevent him ever feeling like his dad's death was his fault. Because it wasn't. It was the Shinnas' fault. It was Stepka's fault.

"We told you this is a safe place," she called back. "*We* were wrong, not you."

I shoulda kept you beside me.

Or your dad here shoulda.

There was so much to do now. And Westermann had to keep doing, keep moving.

"You stay in there," she reminded Gerrit and jogged back to the staircase, climbing it up to Tuccio's corpse, avoiding the blood.

Westermann reached inside his shirt, fingers brushing coarse chest hair, blistered flesh and burned fabric. When she touched a metal chain, she pulled his ID tags out, yanked them hard to snap the chain from around his neck, knelt there weighing them in her palm for a moment. Some people had taken to calling the things "dog tags" like they were called in old-world streamies. Dog soldiers. Dog teams. Dog tags, she figured, was as good a name as any.

Pushing the tags down the inside of one boot, positioning them so they didn't drive her nuts, she wished she'd had time and presence of mind to do the same for the guys from her team. ID tags contained data storage wafers, and many Marines used them to store private, personal messages for loved ones, and sometimes for other members of their platoons or squads they were especially close to. Tuccio had no one to leave a message for—that was widely believed. But her team had. She bore Badillo's last message for his kids in her own mind— it would have been nicer coming to them direct from the wafer in his tags.

"Hackdamn this to hell," she said and returned to Gerrit's room. Other than putting the bottles in the bag and stretching his legs in front of him, the boy hadn't moved.

"A lady said you fell down the stairs?" she said.

He reached along his legs to rub gently at one ankle, flinching, his English faltering as he replied, "I saw the dead Peacekeeper and I scared and fell."

She moved over and teased back his pants leg from the ankle he'd touched. He wore no socks inside his shoes, so she could easily see the discoloration, the swelling. "Can you walk?"

He shook his head. "I'm sorry ... I'm ..." His voice broke, but before he could sob, he caught himself and swallowed and lifted his chin.

Ah shit, kid. May as well cry now. You're gonna do it anyway.

Misinterpreting her expression, he repeated, "I'm sorry."

She touched his chin. "You got nothing to be sorry about. Nothing. Hear me?"

Another swallow. A nod.

"Good. So, I'll carry you. You know what a piggyback is? No? Well, I'm about to show you."

And I'm glad you're a skinny little bugger.

"Before I do, listen up. I gotta tell you something that's real tough for you to hear. Real tough. But you need to know it, and you need to know I'm here for you till the end of this thing. All right? I won't leave you."

Another nod.

A deep breath, then she plunged right in. "Your dad's dead, Gerrit. I wish it wasn't true, but it is, buddy."

She'd thought his face had already been pale beneath its light sunburn, but it seemed to drain of all blood right then. Blood, and emotion. A blank face. A doll's face.

Westermann thought it might be the single worst expression she'd ever seen.

She pressed on. "Happened suddenly. He's a hero, Gerrit. He came to find you and help you but these … these bad guys got him. And he's right outside that door there."

The boy's wide gaze swung to the open mouth of the doorway and fixed there.

"It's your decision, Gerrit, all yours. You wanna see him? Or you wanna hide your eyes when we go past him? Take a minute to think it through. We can—"

"See him," he said hoarsely. "I want to see him." He still stared at the doorway.

She blew out a breath. "All right, then. Gimme your bag." She still had one handgun holstered; she put the loose one into his bag, shouldered it, then got the kid to wriggle to the edge of the mattress.

She carried him in both arms into the corridor, felt his breath against her neck until it caught at the sight of his father. She lowered him carefully onto his butt beside the dead man.

Gerrit put a hand to Stepka's brow, stroked the hair silently for one beat, two, three—then put his hands to his own face, howling.

Shuffling closer, Westermann dumped his bag and dropped to both knees to gather him into her arms, hugging him close against the hard plates of her armor, feeling the bruises from the punches and the bullet, riding out his sobs and pushing away all the soldier-thoughts that told her more bogeys might turn up any sec. If they

184

did, she'd deal with them. This was important, this right here.

For a time, her mind was blank, fizzing with nothing-thoughts. Then it started thinking about the Marines who'd died today. Then it moved on to ID tags and the sad fact there was no one to mourn Tuccio, no one for him to send a final message to.

And then a thought hit her from out of nowhere.

What if he *had* recorded a message on his wafer tag? For whoever might find him if he died out here. And what if the asshole had actually done his job, gathered intel, put it on the tag?

And what if it's useful to me?

She'd have to check it before she left here. There'd been a datareader in the kitchen, undamaged by pirate interference or the firefight. She could tap the wafer to it, scan the files, be done in a minute or two.

But first, there was Gerrit. There was this.

It might have taken five minutes, it might have taken ten, but his weeping was soon spent. At the first sign of him pulling away from her, she released him, but took his chin and raised his face to hers. She didn't really know what to do here, what to say. *Sometimes words come after you start talking,* her dad had told her once. *Sometimes it's better you say anything than nothing.*

"I've got you, kid," she said. "I've got you, all right? Till this thing is done."

He nodded dully. She turned him back toward his father.

"Tell him something."

A long shuddering breath, then he asked, "What do I say?"

Sometimes words come after you start talking.

"Tell him ... Tell him you're gonna see him again one day. And you're gonna make him proud until then. Coz he is gonna be proud of you, Gerrit. Of all the good things you're gonna do. And tell him about all the things you love about him."

A sniffle. "All right."

"And tell him in your language. Yeah?"

"Yes."

"I have to do something quick in the kitchen, so I'll let you talk. But I'll be back real soon, yeah?"

"Yeah." Another deep, shaky breath then Gerrit spoke in Taal as Westermann headed along the corridor. The phrases she heard behind her sounded sure and confident, the boy's tone sober.

In the kitchen, she got her boot up beside the datareader on the counter and pulled out Tuccio's tags. The reader was the generic type, a workplace *fast-look-up* type. No one's personal device, so no passwords or breath prints or retina scans. She thumbed it on, waited till the scan-strip appeared at the top of the screen, held Tuccio's data-tag there and let the software pair the two. A folder appeared onscreen. Three files: a text document titled *Last Will & Test.*, a map file with a long label indicating its geoposition, plus a video file with a numeric label.

Hope I'm not doing something hinky here, Tuccio.

The moment the video file started, Westermann knew she wasn't.

Chapter 13: Video File

"One of the greatest misassumptions of our time is equating pirates' lack of common morality with a lack of intelligence. To have survived for so long and in such conditions, all of the pirate factions have well-proven their intelligence, their resourcefulness and their ability to plan ahead."

Iverson, Cohan & Kalili, *"The Reunification of Human Civilization - a History of Recovery after the Second Dark Age",* Dogstar Press, 2998, page 701

IT WAS strange to look at Tuccio's living face when she'd just been looking at his dead one.

He'd recorded his message in this very room, the bunker kitchen, sitting at one of the tables the pirates had overturned for the firefight. The bookshelf was visible over his shoulder. There were background noises as he got whatever device he'd used to stand in a stable position: people arguing about next steps, someone crying, someone telling her to shut up. Tuccio appeared oblivious to all of it. His face lacked even a speck of emotion. The same with his voice when he started speaking to camera …

"This is important intel for whoever comes in next," he said. "This is just in case the bastards find us here and kill us and someone finds my body. Shit. They might take me somewhere else to kill me—*if* they catch me alive."

"Stop talking like that, Tuccio!" a man demanded, someone in another part of the room.

Tuccio ignored him totally. "So, I better say I'm with the KnowTown staff in the foothills bunker now. The orbital staff went elsewhere, I'm not saying where in case the pirate scum find this. Now. Doctor Kadie reckons the pirates're here for the nukes. Doctor Harkin reckoned they're here for her virus cultures, but she wouldn't say what *they* are. Reckoned she shouldn't have even mentioned 'em." Someone tried to shoosh him off-camera and he gave them a scathing look before continuing. "As if I can't guess what they are. But Harkin drove off from KnowTown in her big ol' car before I got the rest of these idiots onto the train and got 'em here."

Tuccio leaned back in his chair, warming to his story.

"As if they couldn't direct the damn thing here without me. But Harkin didn't give me the option of going with her. Guessin' she went wherever her big-secret lab is. Or else, well, *maybe* she just drove out into the badlands to hide somewhere away from the rest of us … Nah I ain't believin' that. I mean, she's a cow all right, but …"

There was commotion among the scientists, snatching

his attention up and over the camera. His hand snapped forward to cut the recording.

Leaving Westermann starting at a blank screen.

A short and quiet moan: *Nukes. Virus cultures.* "Hack this to hell."

She closed the video file, tapped on the map one. An aerial image and location text she couldn't decode immediately, with stylus-scrawl from Tuccio across the bottom of the picture: *PRC nuke bunker. Sealed.*

Westermann pushed the reader down the counter, then stalked away to lean against the inside of the kitchen entry, breathing hard.

"You wanted to know why they came," she told herself. "Now you do."

PRC nuke bunker. Sealed.

Did that mean the Chinese had stored nukes here and they'd sealed the bunker during the pandemic? Or that Confederation military and scientists had sealed it upon rediscovery? Or something else? How long would nuclear weapons remain viable? Even if they were intact in their underground hidey-hole, the things hadn't been maintained in nine centuries.

"Still enough material probably for a dirty bomb," she told herself. "Or enough uncorrupted data to help 'em reverse-engineer their own weapons."

But ... 'sealed.' She had to hope that meant they couldn't get to it in the time they had. This Harkin's virus research lab might be another thing.

"Day's not over yet, Marine," she said and returned to Gerrit.

The boy was head down beside his father, not

touching him, lost in thought. Or in shock. Westermann dragged his bag over, roused him, made him sling it. In a crouch, she shifted around till her back was towards him.

"Arms around my neck. That's it. Good. Okay, I'm standing up now."

When she was upright, she started moving with one hand holding his leg steady, and the other on her side holster. She was surprised to find that her legs were taking her to the refuge's rear staircase. It seemed she'd already made a decision without consciously thinking it through. The staircase had to lead to the top of the hill. Where the Z-22 was.

I could put him in that train. Get him to KnowTown, maybe find a car there.

I can't do that. They destroyed the other end remotely. And I'd just run into more Shinnas there, anyway.

The Z-22 it is.

At the base of the stairs, she saw she was probably right about them leading all the way up. They rose a very long way, at least twice as far as the other staircase.

"Someone will come back for your dad, but right now we gotta stay away from the Shinnas."

"All right."

Her mind churning with Tucchio's intel, she paused with one boot on the lowest riser, and whispered, "Sono-fabitch," then added, "Don't *you* say that word, kid."

Gerrit sniffed snot up his nose. "Is it bad?"

"Yes."

"Then why did you say it?" His voice was dulled, but it was a relief to her that he'd recovered his grasp of English. His mind was working. He was with her.

"Because I found out some real hinky intel, and it deserves a rude word.

"I don't understand."

She gave his leg a squeeze. "I don't understand half of what I do, so why should you?"

Still, she hesitated, didn't climb. She was talking about cursewords with this kid instead of moving. Because she was tired—just damn tired, and overwhelmed by matters way bigger than her, and her mind was looking for simple things to spin its attention onto so it could stop thinking about the big things, the bad things, the hard things.

But the hard things are what I gotta focus on, she thought with a quiet sigh. She started climbing, immediately irritated by the extra weight of the kid, but committed to bearing it.

I really gotta work out more.

"What is this way?" Gerrit asked.

"Interceptor on top of the hill."

At least two of the bogeys I scratched came out of it. Dunno where the rest of these mutts came from. Musta got dropped off by the bigger ship.

Or else there were more interceptors up top.

"A Z-22? A fighter?"

"*Exactamente*," she replied.

His questions were good. The boy really wasn't withdrawing, wasn't sinking into shock.

No, she thought. *Shock comes later, I guess. When you got time to really second-guess yourself, and overthink things.*

She saw in her mind's eye Badawi, Jeng and Badillo.

To shift her thoughts away from that, and away from

the armor pressing on her bruises, she kept talking. "In BASIC, we took classes to fly runabouts. Long time ago, but I reckon I can get an interceptor moving. And land it near Allie's hide."

She thought, *You shoulda made it here, Jeng. You woulda been perfect for this.*

Her legs were burning when she hit the halfway point. Pausing for breath, she missed something the boy said. "Huh?"

"I said I can fly it."

She started to laugh, turning the laugh into a cough to avoid hurting his feelings. "That's a nice offer, but you're injured."

"I don't need my feet. I only need hands to fly small ships."

Well, the kid did help his dad hard-land a shuttle.

Yeah, but he can't fly a nine-hundred-year-old fighter-interceptor. Surely.

She snorted at that. *And you can?*

"Kid," she said. "I know you spend a lot of time on that simulator game, but—"

"It's not a game. It's a real simulator."

"Yeah. A simulator."

"And I helped Papa fly shuttles since when I was small."

"How small?"

"Even before I remember."

Christ. Really?

"Well, that fighter's an old fighter. It might have very different controls."

Right. And you wanna fly it?

"And the Shinnas let me fly some of their ships," the boy continued, real heat returning to his voice now. "They made me."

"They …?"

"They make all kids learn to do things. They think it's funny. They tease us."

"Hack me. They're completely loco."

"But … I like flying. I'm happy when I fly."

"Listen, Gerrit, even if you know your way around a helm, the text will be in Shinna language."

"I can read some; I told you before."

"Or it could be in PRC Mandarin."

"Please. Can I look at it when we get up there?"

She fell silent and started climbing again: apparently some part of her was committed to giving the kid a shot.

The Shinnas aren't the only ones who're loco.

Her breath was coming hard. She ached everywhere. "You know what, guy? If you can fly it—I mean, if you really can fly it—and I can take a break, I will be forever grateful to ya."

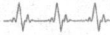

THEY EXITED through a pill box poking out top of the hill. Only one fighter-interceptor sat there, waiting, and no one guarded it. Westermann put Gerrit down so he could sit against the pill box door while she approached. The Z-22's canopy access to the cockpit was positioned just forward of the wings. Once Westermann figured out how to pop it, she found two flight seats, just as Jeng had said there'd be, situated one behind the other.

When she'd helped Gerrit join her on the fuselage, he pointed at the slightly elevated seat at the rear. "That's the pilot's."

That seat was the only one with a direct view through the narrow viewport pane that ran down the middle of the canopy. The forward seat sat too low for that. Both crew—like those aboard almost all larger ships these days—would rely on external cameras and sensor imaging for their vision.

God, I hope they still work. She asked, "Front one's for a gunner?" Or maybe for a passenger, whoever did the actual PRC police work back when these Maoan Z-22s forced ships to land planetside.

Gerrit clarified, "Tactical officer. If the pilot gets hurt, they can fly a little. Also for navigation and comms jacking."

"Oh." Remembering details from high school history, she added, "I guess, after all that computer crap in the 21st century, even the PRC didn't want AIs handling stuff a pilot couldn't, and screwin' things up for both of 'em." She raised a clenched fist, offering a tired grin. "People power, *oi!*"

His brow wrinkled in a frown as he climbed into the pilot's station. Either it wasn't funny, or it made no sense to him. Probably both, she figured.

He spent a couple of minutes recognizing controls and instructions. Also mumbling in Taal. Then he nodded confidently. "I can fly this."

A joke occurred to her, something about a second crash landing today killing them both. But she decided it would be in bad taste this soon after Stepka's death.

Instead, she said, "I'm too beat to argue. We'll try it. Real careful. Test flight. You lift off here and land out in the grasslands."

And after we get you to Allie's, you show me how to fly this thing, and I find that lab. Or the nuke bunker. Wherever the hack they're focusing.

"*Goot*," he said, responding to her plan.

"'Good,'" she corrected him before realizing he was distracted, frowning at the control board and cursing it in Taal. "What now?"

"They changed this one. I think the pilot doesn't want anyone to fly it if he doesn't let them."

"I'm not following ya, kid," she said.

"I need a … a *shleestel*. I don't remember your word. There is a hole here for it."

"A key?"

"Something like that maybe. Something skinny like a … a card. With a … a data piece on it. To go in the hole and start the systems."

Westermann growled, "A goddamn key," and climbed out onto the fuselage. "Have to go back down and search for it."

"I'm sorry." Gerrit shrugged, but his chin had a tremble going.

"Not angry with you, Gerrit. Just with the universe makin' me work harder than I need to. For every damn thing," she added as she lowered herself to the ground.

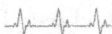

SHE WAS SEARCHING the bodies of the two Shinnas in

pilot gear when the facility rumbled, the floor vibrating beneath her. It lasted seconds only, leaving her shaking her head.

"Just great, universe: let me make it this far then bury me in a damn earthquake."

But there were no further rumbles. And her search continued for a minute more before the key appeared in a flight suit pocket, a long skinny strip like the kid had suggested, with a data chip at one end. She tossed it in the air, caught it and was headed for the stairs again when it occurred to her that the tremor may have been Gerrit starting the flyer's engines, after all. Maybe the kid wanted his own revenge, without her around to stop him.

"Oh, you are *not* leaving me here, you little mutt!"

Taking the stairs two at a time, she chided herself for leaving him alone in the fighter. She forced a fast pace all the way up, muttering and cussing, ribs complaining with each breath, legs burning. And when she burst through the pill box door, she stopped dead, one hand on the door handle, the other drawing her spare sidearm.

A second Z-22 had excited its own vertical landing over toward the edge of the hill, the true source of the rumbling and vibration. A Shinna woman shifted in Westermann's left side peripheral vision, a woman with blue spiky hair, a masculine jaw, and a stubby rifle aimed at the Peacekeeper's head.

And a shaven-headed guy leaned against *her* Z-22, holding Gerrit in front of him with a pocket-sized stun gun pressed to the kid's chest. He could have been the twin of the chub she'd shot on the assault shuttle ramp back on the freighter.

He said, "Gun to the floor."

Jaw clenched, she didn't budge, gaze fixed to his. "You mutts speak English?"

The bald guy's wide shoulders rose and fell in a shrug. But his muzzle never shifted from Gerrit's chest. "Listened to *you* for an 'undred years, lahzzie. Recordings. Comms from your ships. *Put your gun to the floor.*"

Still she resisted, carefully freeing the hand that held the door and raising it in a fist. "Shinnas like killing defenseless people, huh? Freighters that can't shoot back. Children that can't shoot back. That because you're cowards? Weak?"

His frown was a quizzical one, rather than offended. Maybe he couldn't completely follow what she was saying.

She slowed it right down for him. "You like a fight? Well, let's *fight*. I mean, hey, I'm slimmer than you. And I'm sure as hack a lot tireder than you."

A smile split his dirt-caked face, revealing yellow, uneven teeth beneath the beard. "You want *battle* me, lahzzie?"

"Hand to hand. Boot to boot. No guns."

His grin broadened, but he said nothing for the moment.

Westermann jerked her head at the woman beside her. "If I win, she lets me and the boy free. If you win, then okay, but the kid goes free that way too, right? You leave him here."

And while I'm fighting you, maybe Gerrit will have the brains to get your gun and shoot this bitch, then you.

The thought made her feel dirty, like she was leading

197

the kid into some kinda sin, like the religious people called it.

Nah, I didn't lead him into nuthin, she thought angrily. *These assholes did all of that.*

The big, bald guy had been staring her down. He'd been quiet long enough that she was about to dumb it down more when he moved the stun gun away from Gerrit's chest then pushed the boy aside. Gerrit, unbalanced on his injured foot, reached for the fighter fuselage but slid down it anyway until he sprawled in the dirt and the short dry grass. The pirate didn't seem to notice. He nodded once and told Westermann, "You win, she leave him here."

Carefully, deliberately, Westermann lay down her weapon and rose into a fighter's stance, shuffled closer, closing the gap, figuring she may as well get it over.

I'll do it right, not like with Moree. No hackin' around this time.

She pictured what she'd do, getting her plan straight as she edged closer. He wore an e-suit with the helmet off, so a kick in the balls probably wouldn't work. But she could still sweep his legs out from under him. Kneel on his chest. Brain him with that rock there.

And just when she was almost close enough to launch that first leg sweep, she realized he still held his weapon. And his smile had reached his eyes.

He'd never intended to fight her fair and square.

She said, "Oh, you sonofa—"

The Shinna shot her in the chest.

Chapter 14: The Shinna

"When the shenty stared into the eyes of the feral dog, she saw its hunger and she knew her time was over. For nothing in her evolution had prepared her to face this creature. Nothing in her experience had prepared her to face this creature. It was alien to her land and to her world and to her experience. A creature who wanted nothing else but to destroy her completely, to consume her, skin and bone, muscle and marrow.

"And as the creature pressed her down, down, down into the mud and leaned over her and sprayed its hot, awful breath over her, the shenty had one thought. 'Who will protect my little lamb?'"

From *The Feral and the Shenty*,
Westermann's favorite childhood bedtime story.

WESTERMANN GRADUALLY CAME to the realization she was waking up. In some gloomy place. Body slumped. Eyes gummed up. Chin resting on chest. A metallic surface hard beneath her ass. Tightness and tenderness around the left side of her chest as if a horse had kicked her. Hot bile in her throat. Pins and needles in her extremities. Pressure in her temples that pulsed in time with her heartbeat. Dry eyes. Dry mouth.

Something had been wrapped across her torso and shoulders to prevent a slide onto the ground, a slide her body really *really* wanted to do.

Gradually her eyelids came open, crusty with dried tears, but the world remained dark-edged, fuzzy. Glazed.

What ...?

Where ...?

There'd been a hill. A hill with baked soil beneath her boots and harsh sunlight burning her face, and she'd been standing on the hill. With a man and a woman. And there'd been the hiss of a breeze through dry grass. And the man had been speaking.

People were talking here too, down at the end of ... whatever space this was. A manufactured place for sure, a compartment, tight and confined with hard surfaces to bounce the sounds around, a background hum of machinery to muffle them again. *The bunker?* she wondered, beginning to remember, and wishing the memories would stay buried a little longer, give her peace.

Raising her head meant the shoulders moved also—and *that* brought a spasm to her upper ribs, a spike of headache. Spinning head, tight gut, the burn of vomit in the back of her throat, the spasm spreading down the side of her chest ...

Breathe. Breathe.

It took effort to fill her lungs, to insist on pushing against the spasm and the bruising. Westermann kept her head up, blinking until her eyes agreed to focus better, although her vision now spotted with pinpricks of color.

Bastard stunned me.

So this is what it's like on the other end of that.

She couldn't remember the moment he'd fired, but did remember who'd done it now. He'd hit her in the chest; that much was obvious from the way it seemed to have joined-together all the other injuries dealt to that region today.

A fat lot of good that armor bra had done her.

The armor was gone, she realized. All of it. Gloves gone. Boots gone. They'd left her just in her undersuit; something to be grateful for, at least. And they'd harnessed her against a bulkhead from the feel of it, onto the side bench of a passenger cabin, or inside a ship's hold perhaps, leaving the straps loose, allowing her to sag against them. Now that she'd leaned back against the cool steel framing behind her, the pressure on her torso lifted, relaxing the spasm. She could breathe again, though every inhalation hurt like a bitch.

Speaking of bitches, she thought, turning her attention to the far end of this cabin—she was sure it was a cabin now, though her eyes still refused to define it. Two people stood down there, fifteen meters or so back. Talking the shit. Talking in their dumbass pirate lingo. One male, one female. And the female, judging by the fuzz of blue hair on her head, was the one who'd stood by the hilltop pillbox and held a rifle on her.

Yeah, that's you, all right.

Westermann ran her hands over the parts of her undersuit she could reach without effort. Intact. No doubt, that wouldn't last long once they got her back to their mother ship. This thought made her wince more than the fresh wave of vertigo sweeping over her.

She'd been turned to her right to check out the people standing aft. When she moved her head the other way, her vision cleared enough to meet the eyes of a third pirate in the cabin. A short man with a double chin, wearing the kind of gear the Z-22 pilots had worn. This ship's pilot.

What ship was this?

Cargo ship. Inside her head, Gerrit's voice added, *Stomach ship*, his description from earlier that day.

Were they even on Zuchola anymore? How much time had passed?

Enough time to clearly make out this pilot's clown-assed grin turning to a sneer. The man's focus shifted to his right and down. Westermann followed it—and her heart actually fluttered against her ribs like a trapped bird in a cage.

Her thinking came clear. Her eyesight too. And the pains around her body shifted their effect on her, sharpening her up.

Kid!

Gerrit had been positioned at the far end of the same hull-hugging, bare steel bench she'd been dumped on. Up by the cockpit hatch. Harnessed loosely, same as her. Hunched forward, eyes closed, mouth working as he maybe talked to himself.

The pilot caught her eye again, raised a hand to his chest. Westermann could see what he intended.

Don't you —

The back-handed swing caught Gerrit across the forehead. The boy cried out, and reared back so that his head struck an exposed joist. Another short cry.

It brought Westermann half-off her seat, but the harness bounced her straight back down. Her head also struck a joist, drawing laughter from both ends of the cabin. Gerrit had a hand over his brow, jaw trembling. There came a final snicker from the pilot before he turned on his heel and made for the cockpit.

Goddamned bastard. Goddamned bastard, I'll kill you for that.

Leaving the door open, the pilot stepped through a meter-deep divider-room between the cabin and the cockpit proper, a safety lock of sorts with a hatch front and back. Past it, it seemed like there were two chairs in the cockpit: Westermann could see the starboard one where the pilot seated himself. The square of window visible over his shoulder showed pale blue sky.

Still on-planet.

A deep *thunk* shook the back of the cabin; a faint tremor started up in the deck and the seat. The drives initiating.

Still on-planet. But not for hacking long.

Westermann tried catching Gerrit's eye, but all the boy's attention had shifted to the flight area visible through the open hatches. Was he also thinking murderous thoughts? These were the people who'd slain his dad, after all. Surely not—surely a child wouldn't think like she was. More likely, she thought as she gave the cabin better scrutiny, he was thinking how crappy the flight controls looked from his position.

Because the rest of this junk heap looked awful, like it had been hobbled together from bits of other ships over many centuries.

Which probably it had.

The cabin was a long and narrow crew deck.

Stomach ship, Gerrit had said. *Some of their cargo ships carry a big container underneath them and it looks like a stomach.*

This deck would sit up top, separate from whatever container the Shinnas had been filling with Zucholan loot. The portside bulkhead held the steel bench she and Gerrit had been dumped on, a seat long enough for fifteen or so people to sit shoulder to shoulder. The starboard side had a much shorter bench along the back half of it. Random Chinese and European characters had been scrawled or stenciled around the cabin in various colors and sizes. Much of the ceiling insulation—along with the insulation between the exposed joists, stringers, and wall panels— ranged in color from scuffed-up gray to cigarette-stain brown. One patch of wadding along the ceiling was so white—so new it almost glowed by comparison. A toilet station lay off the aft end of the deck, in the bulkhead between the cabin and drive module—and that was it for passenger niceties.

This crew compartment had been built for utility and not for comfort, designed for folks performing a simple job in short-range trips. Less than a day ago, Westermann had been bitching about the discomfort of an assault skiff;

she vowed never again to complain about Confederation ships.

Sure. Like I'll ever see one again.

A side hatch was positioned directly opposite her seat, one that would join with a mating arm from another ship. Even this hatch seemed hinky, secured in place with a simple lock-wheel and flip-latch.

I could open that, now, she thought. *Get the hell out of here with the kid.*

No, you couldn't, snorted Badawi's voice in her head. *Not before they blew your stupid head off.*

Little Miss Blue Hair and her male conversation buddy continued loitering down by the hatch to an aft ladderwell, chatting, ignoring her again. The woman had stowed her rifle hack-knew-where, and simply wore a long Shinna handgun at her hip.

Also, she had a shenty skull clipped to one of her suit pouches.

Westermann's heart fluttered again, for a new reason.

That ...

Her temples pounded harder.

... is ...

Her teeth ground together.

... mine!

If she got this harness off and got down there, she could rip that skull free and jam its hooked beak into Blue Hair's carotid—then slash it across the other guy's eyes.

She had one of her buckles unclasped before reality set in: make the wrong move here and she was dead. Dead— leaving Gerrit friendless and defenseless. They had no *need* for her beyond payback for the pirates she'd already neutralized. Push these assholes too far, and they'd figure it was easier to kill her now and be done with it.

It was agonizing to settle back against the hull framing, to force herself to do nothing besides letting this be, but there wasn't much choice.

Yet.

Above her a PK helmet had been stored in the stownetting along the ceiling. There were others in the netting further forward, too. She counted four in total. The bowl above her wasn't hers from back on *Artemis*. Wasn't Jeng's or Badawi's or Badillo's. And why would it be? All of their armor had been torched along with their bodies on Stepka's cargo runner. This one had some other PK's nickname stenciled along the jawline, half out of view. *MANG* was all she could make out. Some other PK from some other raid. And that poor hacker hadn't made it.

If she stretched hard, she might reach it and prod it out the side of the netting, or simply angle it to tap and activate the HUD inside. It might help her transmit. It might help her trans*late*, she thought with a glance to the pair of talkers. She could listen in to what they were saying.

Sure, sneered the smartass voice in her head, *like it has Shinna language progged into it.*

And even if it had been re-progged for some reason by Shinnas, the fact was, that if Westermann could hear the audio, the pirates would hear it too.

Hack.

It was better for the moment to observe the pair who stood aft, study them for clues and opportunities.

The male standing with Little Miss Blue Hair wasn't

someone Westermann remembered seeing before. A guy with a pencil neck poking from the relative bulk of his stained and scruffy e-suit. With his thin fringe of hair around an egg-shaped head, his tablet clasped beneath one armpit, and his data-pen stabbing the air as he spoke, he was every streamie's stereotype of a nerdy scientist.

Three, thought Westermann. Just these three had come in here with her. *All that's left?* she wondered. There'd be a couple more probably flying the Z-22s offworld. But it wasn't many. As she got her heartrate under control, wriggling this way and that to test and stretch and prime her aching muscles, Westermann counted cabin harnesses. Ten along her bench, six along the other. No doubt all had been in use when the hauler came down to Zuchola; hardly any would be used for the return trip to the gunboat—and that was on her.

Westermann blew out a breath. These animals had unspeakable things planned for her. And she could take it, she *would* take it, without giving them the satisfaction of screaming or weeping.

But to Gerrit, they'd do worse.

Because they would turn the kid into one of them.

That thought turned her hollow, made her mutter curses.

Her vision had definitely improved: not so speckly, not so dark-edged. And she could inhale more deeply against the tightness where the stunner had struck her ribs. The harness straps remained a major irritant. One of them—tighter than the others—slipped up and down across her ribs with every breath no matter which way she turned or wriggled. The two pirates noticed her squirming, so she quit that and slumped again.

Not so long ago, Jeng the Noog had watched her wiggle and cuss like she'd just been doing. She recalled his concerned expression, the reassuring smile he'd offered her when *he'd* been the one who was nervous. The picture of his kind and innocent face brought her some comfort even now. There were evil bastards in the world; there were also the exact opposite.

Until the evil bastards kill 'em.

Gerrit faced her way. She gave him some Jeng: a reassuring smile, a wink, a thumbs-up. The boy nodded, biting his lip to control its trembling. Then his gaze shifted past her and his eyes widened.

The commander climbed out of the aft ladderwell, the bald guy who'd stunned her. Both of the Shinnas back there called him "Willen." Westermann could think of other names for this mutt. He secured the hatch across the ladderwell, tightened the lock-wheel, and inserted a thick lock-pin.

The other two Shinnas dumped their asses on the aft bench seat. The scientist guy fumbled with a harness; the woman snaked one arm though another without bothering to pull it fully over her. Willen stopped in front of the scientist-type and handed him a small cooler box, big enough to carry four long-neck beer bottles.

Tasting stomach juice again, Westermann thought, *That ain't beer in there.*

Among the many common CUSET-era pictograms that the DCHC had adopted was the one clearly stenciled on the side of that box. To her, the symbol had always looked like three sets of horns, pointed in three directions, laid on top of a circle.

Biohazard.

Tuccio was right.

And if it wasn't PBT in that box, it would be something just as bad.

Willen stomped halfway up the cabin, barked a command at the cockpit and gripped the ceiling stow-netting as the ship lifted off with a lurch. For a moment, g-forces pressed Westermann hard onto the bench. Then came relief as the arti-grav belatedly kicked in. Nodding in satisfaction at the pilot's instant obedience, Willen wandered back down to join the other two. The cabin had been growing warm while the ship sat on the Zucholan plain, but an air handler started up now that the engines were operational. Cool air flowed from a vent above the cockpit door, dropping cabin temp immediately, the abrupt chill biting into Westermann's cut cheek and her bare feet. The insulated body suit would grant some protection if the cabin insulation wasn't up to scratch. But if the extreme cold of space seeped inside—or that air handler didn't warm up by quite a few degrees—the kid would also find it rough, dressed in his loose-fitting ship-clothes.

The pirates didn't care about air temperature, though their conversation came out on puffs of steam now. They had e-suits, gloves, boots. The ship shook like crazy as it rose through the atmosphere, but the Shinnas also seemed to trust their rickety ride just fine, leaving their helmets stowed up in the ceiling netting.

And they were more interested in the box than

anything. Westermann's breath caught in her throat when the scientist steadied it on his knees and began unclipping the lid.

"Are you serious!" she shouted at him.

The three pirates glanced her way. Willen made some kind of joke. The others laughed.

And the scientist flipped open the lid.

It was like watching someone open a hatchway to hell and reach inside for a demon. A demon that itched to kill everyone onboard, then jump onto whatever ship found them later where it would kill *that* crew too. Westermann shouted obscenities at the top of her lungs, but was forced to fall silent when Willen patted the stunner in his shoulder holster. Her head felt swollen with the increase in blood pressure. Her ribs and sternum ached. And her stomach was leaden with dread.

The scientist drew out a sample container or analyzer, a device the size of his hand with a small datascreen set into the side. Its ends were glass caps—Westermann couldn't see anything inside it, but didn't need to. The thing definitely held something, judging by the way the skinny man fussed with it, brushing his data-pen against the device's small screen.

Bastards probably wanna test it on me.

A fresh chill ran up her back.

Or Gerrit, she thought, imagining the boy injected with a virus that made his organs bleed before eventually liquifying. Imagining the alternative: these psychopaths simply brutalizing and enslaving him for the rest of his days. It was better that Gerrit died a quick and instant death, better they both perished here instead of suffering at the hands of these animals—if she could somehow blow the transit hatch across from her.

And how'm I gonna do that? The lock-wheel and latch that secured it wouldn't come open quickly enough.

In her mind, she heard the voice of Sergeant Judah again: *"You got time to think of a second or third option? Do it. They're probably better than the first idea you had."*

And there *was* another way here, specifically a way for the kid to dodge death. It would mean getting him into the cockpit, locking it off and finding a way to vent this compartment whether she made it in there with him or not.

The transit hatch wasn't sophisticated enough to be controlled from up in the flight area.

Then we'll fly around with prisoners in back.

What, for fifty hours? grumbled the smartass voice. *With these chubs dreaming up ways to break you outa there?*

"Shit," she hissed again, and dug deep into her memories of BASIC, reaching for more of Judah's wise words.

In her memory, Judah had her and a dozen more recruits out in woodlands on Pride of Mao, and he was bawling at them, *"You think. But you don't over think. The parts of the solution are often scattered all around you, out in plain sight. You think just enough to assemble them into the solution you need — then you act."*

And with that, she saw it. The two sealable hatches between the cockpit and cabin. The join across the middle of the anteroom, running through the floor and up the wall that she could see from here. Motorized fasteners had been clamped all round this join, stitching it together. The cockpit was designed to be jettisoned in an emergency. It might have chutes or even retro-thrusters to help it land if ejected in atmosphere.

If she could get herself and Gerrit in there, they could return the ship to Zucholan atmosphere, cut the engines, blow the cockpit clamps, and let the entire back section fall from the sky while she and the kid drifted free.

If they could make it there before Willen the commander drew his stunner, that was. Gerrit was still completely buckled in. If she made a dash for it, releasing his restraints would lose far too much time. She blew out a tired and frustrated breath—and her eye caught on a new detail she hadn't seen earlier ...

The damn cargo ship kept shuddering like a storm-scared shenty as it pushed up through the atmosphere. Across from her, a long bolt rattled in the exposed bulkhead frame beside the transit hatch, loose in its hole. Westermann smiled at it.

Well, hello, beautiful.

The plan had just become clearer—and longer. Get the bolt, release Gerrit from his harness, get the cockpit door closed behind them, punch the pilot in the temple with the bolt, don't get zapped while doing any of it. That last part was the biggest problem. Rubbing the ache in her chest, Westermann realized that simply running for the front of the ship wouldn't cut it: she had to take the fight *to* these three in the cabin before she'd have any chance of locking them in here.

Besides, she thought with a hard stare at the blue-haired woman, *I want my skull.*

With her head lolling to the side, Westermann played up her exhaustion while checking on her captors. Willen stood over the pair at the back, hand on the netting above him, making conversation, completely disinterested in her. She stretched her legs and wiggled her toes. If anyone was watching, it would shift the focus off her hands as she released another of the remaining harness buckles.

The ship's shaking subsided now. Blue Hair got off her seat and put a boot to the opposite bulkhead, stretching her hamstrings. And blocked Willen's view.

Westermann flipped the final buckle on her harness and pushed to her feet, stumbled across the aisle and into the bulkhead by the transit hatch, turned her back to the pirates and pulled out the bolt, palmed it. The predictable shouting started up behind her. She rested one arm on the bulkhead and pivoted toward it, sagging with a weakness and weariness she was only partly faking. The blue-haired woman stormed toward her, wearing a malicious half-smile that telegraphed her intentions pretty well. The gun remained holstered; she was buying Westermann's act and making ready for some rough treatment of her prisoner.

If it's the direct approach ya want ... Westermann thought as the pirate drew close.

"I'm sick," she moaned. Holding her stomach, she pretended to dry retch, then added hoarsely, "Need the shitter."

Blue Hair understood that English just fine, hesitating just out of reach of someone she expected to puke, half-turning to bark a question back at Willen, and presenting her right side with its holster toward Westermann, a holster lacking a safety strap across the pistol's grip.

Idiot, Westermann thought and grabbed at the weapon left-handed.

The pirate reacted as most people might, both her own hands reflexively going for the lethal weapon at her hip. Which positioned her arms down, against and across her body. Which left her face unprotected.

Westermann had already flipped the bolt up between her first two fingers, and curled a fist around it. With this, she swung high. Aimed for the right eye. Hit it. Warm fluid misted against her hand as she withdrew it. Blue Hair recoiled, too shocked yet to scream, twisting away, both hands snapping up to her face now. Westermann dropped the bolt and plucked out the handgun, clubbed Blue Hair with the muzzle. Something sizzled into the transit hatch. Another stun-bolt hit the pirate woman on her way to the deck. Westermann had been intending to threaten the others with the pistol. But the incoming fire kicked in her instincts, those instincts raising the pistol. She squeezed, watched Willen flinch and clasp his arm and gasp with surprise as his stunner slipped from his hand. It bounced off his boot, skipped across the deck and under the bench seat near him.

Westermann put her back to the transit hatch, stabilizing, trying to watch both ways. Gerrit had half his restraints unbuckled.

"*Pilot!* Get out ...!" She bit off the command because he'd already surfaced, standing in the cockpit anteroom with his hands by his sides and his jaw hanging open. She leveled the gun at him. His shoulders fell in resignation as she waved him out of there with the gun.

When he drew level with Gerrit, the kid made an

awkward crawl along the bench seat past him, before putting his good foot to the deck and limping into the cockpit. Westermann hadn't needed to tell him where to go.

Smart kid.

Another head-check ensured Willen wasn't stooping for his stunner and didn't have a hold-out weapon. She ducked and snapped the chain holding the shenty skull to Blue Hair's suit, raised the keepsake to her lips, squeezed it inside her jumpsuit where it scratched her skin below a collar bone.

When the pilot was near, she made him edge past with his hands on his head while she stepped up onto the bench to keep her distance.

They were almost out of this.

So close, so close ...

"Gerrit, you hear me?" she called.

"Yes."

"You tell me where that gunboat is, how far off."

"I'm already looking. It's far away. I think they want to meet with it near the leappoint to save time."

"Far away," she said to herself, climbing down off the bench as the pilot kept moving aft. "Things are looking better."

There was a chance she wouldn't need to kill these doghackers after all. Four captured Shinnas would be an intel jackpot for Naval Command. She met Willen's gaze, saw the grudging respect in his eyes despite the fact she'd winged him. Perhaps *because* she'd winged him. Blood seeped between the fingers clutching his injured arm. She was about to ask him to find where her bullet had ended up, because it sure hadn't breached the hull. Before she could, the scrawny scientist leaned around his commander.

And made things worse.

To Westermann, he'd been the least dangerous person on the boat. Only dangerous thing about him had been that sampler gadget he'd been handed. But the man had a pocket stunner of his own. He released a flash of energy to spear past her with a buzzing sound. Reflexively again, she fired back. Just once. Once was enough. Belatedly, Willen dropped onto the bench seat and out of the way. But the firefight was over. The scientist sank to his knees with a red stain spreading languidly from a hole in his e-suit.

And a tiny cloud of aerosol hung in the air between his face and Willen's.

The scientist lifted something in his non-dominant hand and blinked at it.

The sample gadget. Shattered at one end.

Two things flashed through Westermann's mind in the three seconds she stood there with her mouth hanging open …

The cabin airflow was moving past her from the air handler and toward that broken container, keeping her safe.

And whoever came into contact with that small cloud of biohazard was one hundred per cent screwed.

The pilot bawled out a wordless exclamation of horror and reversed direction toward Westermann.

And Westermann fled. Pounding up the aisle and into the anteroom. Slapping the door control. Vaulting the final meter into the cockpit and slapping the control there, too.

She whirled and put her face to the door, doing her best to watch through two windows in doors set two meters apart. Blue Hair was still down and motionless. The pilot was scrabbling for a helmet from the ceiling netting. The scientist had toppled onto his side, his broken sampler either under or behind him now.

"Gerrit," she snapped. "Find a way to test our air for pathogens."

"What-o-gems?"

"Just … check the board for an air quality reading or something."

Had the front-to-rear airflow been strong enough to prevent that crap spreading toward her? Once more, her gaze snagged on Willen's. The pirate commander stared back at her from beyond the scrambling pilot, his eyebrows raised and a resigned expression on his face.

"Found it," Gerrit reported. "Air good in here. *Is* good. The cabin, uh, there's no air quality reading for back there."

"No bigs," she said, still unable to break away from the window. "I know it's bad. You in control of this shitbox?"

He grunted affirmation.

"Any Z-22s on sensors?"

A pause, then: "I don't see any."

"Keep an eye out."

In the cabin, the pilot had seated himself close to the cockpit outer hatch, fitting his helmet well away from the broken virus container. Willen got to his feet, his damaged arm forgotten. The area around the hole in his suit was stained red. He stooped. Picked up the broken virus holder. Considered it for a few seconds. Shrugged and tossed it over his shoulder. On steady feet, he came forward as far as the transit hatch.

From the middle of the aisle where Westermann could see him clearly, Willen met her gaze. Nodded. Leaned sideways and worked at something by the hatch ...

The ship rocked violently.

Beyond the anteroom's windows, the cabin became chaos, a momentary maelstrom of misted air and flailing bodies and churning gear before utter stillness back there.

"What of the hack was that?" Gerrit demanded.

The poor attempt at cussing made Westermann smile. The boy had twisted in his chair toward her. She took the seat beside him and gently punched his arm. "That's a bad word to use, kid."

"Hack?"

She cuffed him again. "Exactly. No more swearing from you."

"But what happened?"

"What happened is we don't have any assholes in the cabin no more."

He frowned a moment, then puffed out his cheeks. "Isn't *assholes* a bad word?"

"*I* can use bad words," she said and closed her eyes, relaxing against the headrest. "I'm a hacking Marine."

SHE STILL HAD Blue Hair's handgun which she stowed in a pouch beneath her chair.

The cockpit *was* built to jettison in an emergency, as she'd suspected—probably part of some pirate *everyone-for-themselves* code. There'd turned out to be no need for it. Though reentry was tricky for Gerrit with a hatch open and the ship's weak shields, he managed it.

With the ship shuddering from high altitude wind resistance, and thankful for her life, she asked him, "Any ideas where we should land?"

"Near Allie's place."

"You can find it?"

"I think so. I … We should get my papa too."

"We should," she said. "We won't leave him. But we'll leave it another twelve hours or so, yeah? Leave it late enough to stop the Shinna gunship or Z-22s coming back for us."

"All right. Yes."

They were on the night side of the planet now, approaching the terminator. The day catching up with her, she yawned. "Gerrit?"

"Yes?"

"You're a damn fine pilot, you know that?"

"Thank you."

"Better than most of the skiff pilots I've flown with."

"They're bad?"

"Oh, they're bad, all right." She yawned again, then added, "And you're a damn good kid. Your papa is proud of you."

He pressed his lips together, accepting that, processing it. Then he replied, "You are a damnhack good Marine."

"Hey. What I tell you about bad language?"

He grinned at that. Westermann needed a checkover by a medic. She needed a meal and a drink, a shower and a long, deep sleep.

But seeing this kid smile was better than any of it.

Chapter 15: Warship

We are rapidly approaching the Fourth Millennium. It is the authors' firm hope that humanity has now entered the beginning of a golden era, in spite of the continued presence of factions who push their own agendas. Our government is firmly rooted in democratic ideals. Crime rates and military skirmishes across member worlds are in fast decline. Our Confederation military is inclined to enact peace rather than abuse power. And the common prosperity of all citizens is evidenced to be on the rise.

We can surely be optimistic that the next millennium of human life and human endeavor will be underpinned by common sense, common empathy and the pursuit of common progress. And, above all, that our species will enjoy peace at last.

Iverson, Cohan & Kalili, *"The Reunification of Human Civilization - a History of Recovery after the Second Dark Age"*, Dogstar Press, 2998, page 1526

EIGHTY-EIGHT HOURS LATER.

THE CHAIRS in *Valiant*'s mess were soft. Too soft.

Westermann couldn't get comfortable in any of them, though she'd tried several. They left too much space between her hips and their arms, making her slouch when she wanted to sit straight. And her experiences since boarding the assault skiff several days earlier had left her with a weird kind of muscle memory, so that she reached for a harness every time she sat anywhere new.

Not the chairs' fault, she guessed.

Wriggling her butt back in the latest chair she'd chosen, Westermann sipped coffee, and tried to focus. A small kit bag lay on the table alongside her fifth cup of coffee, a new bag with fresh and basic personal gear to replace the kit she'd lost on *Artemis*. A pad sat in front of the kit bag. A paper pad. Official Confederation Navy paper with official Confederation Navy letterhead topping each page. She'd been at this task for three hours —and only now did she feel close to getting it right.

During those three hours, maybe three dozen people had come through the mess room, eating and chatting and leaving again. Navy spacers. Techs. A couple of *Valiant*'s Peacekeepers. Westermann had been aware of their stares. She'd been aware she was the topic of their conversations, whenever their speech dropped in volume and the tone took on a hushed intensity. And she'd acknowledged none of it. Not even when another PK had patted her back in passing, a gesture of solidarity and acceptance: *I see you, I respect you, I got you.*

In the lulls when she'd been alone, Westermann had wandered to the servery, topped up her coffee or water, nabbed another sandwich or apple. And she'd kept on with the work at hand, her final mission before departing this damned, cursed star system.

She drummed her fingers on the paper for a moment, and had to admit that this letter she'd written, this *version*, was the best she could manage. It would do the job. Badillo's parents wouldn't judge her by her writing style or spelling or choice of words. She could only hope what she'd written brought them a tiny bit of comfort.

The final words above her signature read,

"He said to tell you he loved you. He died without pain and suffering. But he saved my life and the life of a child. Your son died a hero."

One small lie mixed in with great truth.

It would do. It was enough.

And it now gave her a template for the letters to Jeng's mother and to Badawi's wife and kid.

Leaning back and stretching, she realized that someone stood a meter from her shoulder. They'd probably been standing there a while. She startled, half-turning in the chair. An officer. And not just any officer.

Commander Dilshad Farahaji. The *Valiant*'s Executive Officer. The woman was a smiler. Also thirty-something, as tall as Westermann, and impeccably groomed.

The chair scraped on tiles as Westermann boosted to her feet. The pen rolled off the table. She saluted. "Sir!"

Farahaji made a calming gesture and pulled out the chair beside Westermann's. "May I?"

"Of course, sir. It's your ship, sir."

"I think the captain might disagree with that." She turned the chair side-on, lowered herself into it, crossed her legs. "Sit, Private. Relax, please."

Westermann did as told, angling her chair to better face the senior officer.

Farahaji's eyes did not dart about the compartment at the handful of crew spread around other tables. But she leaned a few degrees closer, lowering her voice. "We have something to discuss before you bounce out."

Westermann shifted in her seat. "Uh … Oh-kay, sir."

"Now that your inquiry and debrief are done, the captain and myself are in agreement that Private Denise Westermann is a trustworthy woman. So, I'm comfortable telling you this and trusting you'll keep it to yourself for the time being. As per protocols, the supply ship you'll travel on will carry dispatches out-system. The captain is including a very special messagepack among them, one for Naval Command: a request for the Exclusion Zone to be bolstered. And a request for *Valiant* to fly to Pollux where we can find that observation post the Shinnas have there, extract those child prisoners they still have, and interrogate the bastards who've been keeping them. Haas and Stepka's associates, too. What do you think would be the main point of that interrogation?"

Westermann swallowed. It was highly unusual for a Navy commander to chat with a PK private, let alone share such information. Now she wanted her to make guesses about it? She answered, "I guess you wanna locate the Angelview system?"

"Correct. And once we've located it, we'll hunt down our new friends, the Shinna Caldones." Her expression darkened. "And that damn carrier-gunship."

The one that got away, Westermann thought, feeling her own face tighten with hatred.

"You find 'em, sir, and you pound 'em to atoms."

"How about *we* pound them into atoms?" The XO crossed her arms.

"Sir?"

"It's a job offer, Westermann. We could use a Marine with your recent experience and ... well, your recent achievements. Of course, it's highly unusual to add a PK to the existing contingent instead of swapping one out. But if we go to Angelview, our entire mission will be kind of unusual. Of course, you may prefer to remain with the reorganized Zuchola blockade group—"

"No. I'd rather finish the job those bastards started than go back to sitting on my ass. Sir."

"Bastards, indeed," Farahaji said quietly. Though she remained leaning forward, her gaze shifted away as she stared into her own thoughts. "This may signify a shift in policy toward ferreting out and eradicating these clans —*finally*—rather than waiting for them to attack us. Although, that policy shift may be a little late in coming. Shortly before we received *Artemis*'s distress signal, we'd had word of a pair of CUSET-era corvettes leaping in close to the *Assured*'s current station, scanning her, and leaping out again."

"Seriously?"

"Approximately ten days ago. Out of nowhere. They were thought to be Clan Lobos. But it makes me wonder now if two such pirate incidents so close together are a coincidence, or if the corvettes were Shinnas, and the animals have more actions planned."

"Maybe the clans have gotten together, sir. Maybe they're planning some kind of push all over."

"Hack, let's hope not. I'm not the only one who'd really like to get on the front foot with this."

Westermann's mind turned to the diplomatic talks that Allie had told her about. Did Farahaji know about them? "There's plenty of pirates still holed up in Xerxes system, isn't there?"

"We think there is, but until Xerxes' nine planetary governments invite us in, we can't start firing particle beams and missiles around their star system." Her expression said she'd go do exactly that tomorrow if someone allowed her.

A pause while the XO lapsed into thought, and Westermann waited for her to rouse herself and continue leading the conversation. When she did, Farahaji said, "I see you're hard at work writing to your teammates' families."

Westermann moved the pad around the table. "Yes, sir. I think I've got it straight what to say. Took a while."

"Worst duty there is. I'm glad you volunteered to do it. It'll mean a lot to their loved ones."

"Are you sure I can't write to Sgt. DeLuca's wife, too?"

"That's the captain's duty. DeLuca was a team leader. Damn protocols, huh?"

"Yes, sir."

Another pause before Farahaji cleared her throat. "So, being clear, you're taking the job with us?"

Westermann hesitated, biting her lip a second. "Would it be possible I join *Valiant* at Pollux?"

"Of course. I'll arrange it. You go home, see your father, recuperate. Two weeks enough?"

"Absolutely, sir."

The XO's gaze flicked to the kit bag and then to the note pad. "There's no hurry to finish that. Take that with you, finish it when you're outbound. Supply ship docks in thirty, boarding in forty-five."

Farahaji stood. Westermann copied her.

The XO leaned in. "No one hears about what happened here, Private. You've obviously been told this, but I'm absolutely making sure you understand the expectation. It applies whether you remain in the service or you leave it. You tell no one. Not your family. Not your lover. Sober or drunk, you never speak a word of this to any unauthorized party."

Westermann had stiffened, offended. "I can keep my jaw shut."

"And I believe you. Over the next month or two, however, you better get used to other higher-ups repeating this same message. And I'd advise you to give exactly that same response."

Epilogue: Arrivals

"In the early years of the Democratic Confederation of Human Colonies, inter-system travel increased dramatically. During this period, the Centauri Federal Government placed its largest transfer hubs well away from the planet. The intention was to thin out large-ship traffic from the planet's near orbit."

A Student's Encyclopaedia of Colonized Space, Grace City Publishing, 13th Edition, 3001

FORTY YEARS BACK, the Pyramus Transit Hub had been completed and parked five-thousand kilometers above the surface of Pyramus Famulus, Centauri's smaller moon. With an immense cylinder at its core, the station hosted a berthing ring at each end which, Westermann thought, made it look like a giant free-weight left hanging out in space.

The south berthing ring—the one at the end closest to the moon's surface—was reserved for military or diplomatic transit. Westermann's supply ship docked here, and she and Gerrit disembarked along with their naval escort. With Gerrit limping from his recent ankle strain, the group crossed the docking tube and entered Pyramus Hub's "Southern Arrivals Terminal." This inner wedge of the berthing ring contained the standard sets of waiting chairs, food kiosks, and information boards. Bored-looking travelers browsed the kiosks while keeping an eye on the boards.

Local time out this side of Centauri was late afternoon. According to Confederation Navy Ship Time, it was just after 0400. Westermann and Gerrit stifled yawns as the two Navy officers pointed them to a row of chairs, which meant a minor delay while the officers confirmed travel arrangements for the next leg of Gerrit's transit to Pollux.

Westermann wore off-duty duds now—loose trousers, ankle-high sneakers, a waist-length travel coat over a black tee. Her kit bag lay on the floor between her shoes. The shenty skull formed a comforting pressure against her skin beneath the tee, strung on a gold chain that Allie had given her upon parting.

Light East Centauran jazz played over the terminal speakers, and Westermann felt a welling of nostalgia.

Almost home.

A goofy grin began forming on her face, but it wilted when she saw that Gerrit's eyes shone with a different emotion.

She slid down in her chair until they were the same height, then bumped his shoulder with hers. "Don't cry,

Mr. Fighter Pilot. I need you to be the brave guy you were on Zuchola."

"Okay."

"Things have been bad for you, but they get better from here."

"Okay."

She winced at his tone. "You don't sound so sure."

Refusing to look at her, he said, "I don't want to leave you."

Westermann swung an arm up over his head then grabbed him by the back of the neck and squeezed in comradely fashion. "Hey, guy. You and me got different jobs. I'm a Marine. You're a pilot. We got different responsibilities and different places to be."

The boy did not resist the physical contact, but neither did he acknowledge it. "It's not fair. I want to stay with you."

Westermann sighed and let him go, looping the arm back over and clasping her hands on her lap. For a while, she tried to think of something wise to say. When nothing came to her, she asked a question instead.

"Do you remember your mom?"

"Yes." He delivered the word with the right amount of *what-a-dumb-question* to bring the smile back to Westermann's face.

"She a nice person or a bad person?"

"Nice."

"She love you?"

He did look at her then, a sharp glance, like he knew where this was headed. "Yes," he admitted.

"Do you want to see her again?"

"Yes."

"Then that's what you're doing. She's the one you belong with. And she needs you, Gerrit. You're all she's got now, right?"

"Right." He looked at her again and this time his eyes shone with affection. "But I'll miss *you*."

Westermann nodded. "That's normal. For friends to miss each other. But, hey, I'm not lying when I say I'll see you again. My next leave rolls around in six or seven months. And I am absolutely coming to visit you."

Even if I gotta bribe Farahaji into letting me off Valiant.

"You can show me your town. I'll take you and your ma to see all the interesting places around your world."

If it has any. She was pretty sure Pollux didn't.

"*Or* I could ask the Navy to fly you back here and I'll show you round Centauri. Would you like that?"

"Yes."

They fell into companionable silence, people-watching. When the male and female lieutenants reappeared from a side office, Gerrit turned to her.

"Westermann?"

"Yeah, kid?"

"Thank you for saving me."

She grunted. "It means a lot you think I did that. Really, it does. But … You know how action streamies always have a hero? Well, the hero in your story is your dad. Without him, you'd still be a prisoner of the Shinnas. Your dad risked everything to get you safe. He got you out, he got you as far as he could—and now it's your turn," she added as she stood and gestured for him to rise with her. Brushing the lump of shenty skull with her fingers, she said, "You get to take your life as far as it can possibly go from here. Make him proud. Make us all proud, kid."

She straightened and saluted him.

Soberly, he saluted her back.

As the Navy officers drew near, she bent close and whispered, "You don't salute Privates. You only salute stiff collars like them."

Gerrit grinned.

"Private, your shuttle's arriving now at Gate 12 on the far side of the ring," the female lieutenant announced. Westermann had shared a long transit with the woman, but she had a forgettable name. And Westermann had forgotten it. To Gerrit, the woman said, "Transport to Pollux leaves in thirty minutes. We'll take a travelator along the main station hub, then board at the north ring. Have you ever been on a travelator before?"

Gerrit shrugged.

"Well, this one's fast. But you can still see out the windows and down to the moon below. Won't that be fun?"

"Yes," the boy answered without enthusiasm.

Westermann imagined he was thinking, *If you want fast, try hard-landing an assault shuttle*. She turned the boy and hugged him to her. Firmly. Briefly. Then she separated and fixed him with a stern look.

"The lieutenants will look after you all the way. Don't give 'em any crap, okay? And give your mom the biggest hug you can when you see her. *And* send me a messagepack to tell me you're all right."

He frowned. "Where ... Where do I send ...?"

"We'll provide those details," said the male lieutenant. Westermann realized she'd forgotten his name too. The man stepped away and gestured for the boy to follow.

Gerrit flashed a final mock salute at Westermann, smiled shyly and joined the man. The woman gave her a nod goodbye. Westermann gave *her* a proper salute.

And that was that. The trio were headed for the lift to the travelator, leaving her alone.

She waited for Gerrit to look back. He didn't. Eventually, he entered the lift and vanished when the lieutenants' bodies blocked him.

"I'll see ya, kid," she said. "Just not in an Exclusion Zone next time."

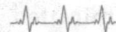

SHE STOOD AT GATE 12, bouncing on the balls of her feet. The shuttle, they'd told her, was a small one. A twelve-seater. About the length and width of *Artemis*'s assault skiff, she figured. It had docked while she'd walked around the terminal, but its small cohort of passengers had yet to disembark. After they did, there'd be a twenty-minute delay while station crew performed turnaround maintenance and preflight checks. After that, she could board.

Until then, she *could* sit to wait. But she'd done enough sitting since leaving Zuchola.

Besides, before disembarking from the supply ship, the lieutenants had told her a surprise awaited her on this shuttle, one the Navy had organized for her, one that would make the trip planetside more enjoyable.

And she was pretty she sure she knew what it was.

She bounced on the balls of her feet some more.

Eventually, the docking gate opened. A flight attendant came out and positioned herself to deliver thank yous as the passengers filed past.

Two government types in ruffled suits emerged first, chatting about sports.

A stout woman in similar clothes to Westermann came next. The woman held her shoulders back and clutched her bag tight in one fist. She strode confidently and wore a *don't-mess-with-me* expression. Westermann recognized another PK when she saw one. She caught the woman's eye. They exchanged nods.

Next out were three short-assed junior Navy spacers, dragging their heels as they returned to duty.

And then a man appeared, pumping the hand of the flight attendant, thanking her warmly in badly broken English. A short man, with broad shoulders and a big head made bigger by its fuzzy mane of graying hair and thick hedge of beard around the jaw.

Westermann felt her heart melt within her and took a couple of stumbling steps his way.

He saw her, his face lit up, and he ran to her in a funny kind of old-man waddle he'd developed since she'd last seen him. "Denny!"

"Dad!" she grinned and wrapped him in her arms.

Dictionary of DCHC slang, locations and terminology

AH: Artificial Habitat, another term for space stations.

Arti-grav: artificial gravity used aboard ships, stations and sometimes asteroids. (Also called shipgrav in the DCHC era.)

Bad Times: the dark age during which humanity's space colonies were separated because of the PBT virus's destruction of populations and civilization (approx. 2145-2910, although individual worlds and planetary regions began recovery earlier than 2910).

bowl: Marine slang for suit helmet.

Castor and Pollux: the two habitable planets of the Dioscurin system (not to be confused with the star originally called Pollux, and the collection of stars called Castor in the constellation Gemini).

chub: an insult, Centauran origin, pre-Confederation era, meaning obscure.

Centauri: Humanity's first settled planet and the third of the original worlds to form the DCHC in the 2980s. At the beginning of the early 31st century, Centauri remains predominantly an agricultural world.

CUSET: Technically the name of a legal document, now the common name for anything to do with the **Corporate Union** who were the major explorers and settlers of space in the 22nd century.

DCHC: Democratic Confederation of Human Colonies
e-suit: environment suit, space suit. Marines wear armored versions of this called combat suits.

Hack/-ing: an expression of profanity, thought to refer to the 21st crimes of spying on individuals and stealing their identity/money via digital means, thus violating their persons.

janky: 30th century Centauran slang for sleepy, out-of-sorts or dizzy.

Millennialists: a common name for various late-30th-century cults. Some Millennialist sects were religious in nature, others secular, some pacificist, some violent. Many were doomsday cults, while a handful had been founded on conspiracy theories (for example that the PBT virus had actually been digital technology, and that 30th century information technology was a form of toxic alien life). Most of these cults faded away by the year 3008.

noog: Shortened version of "new guy" or "new gal".

pendejo: idiot, dirtbag (Spanish).

PK: Peacekeeper, Confederation Marine.

prog: a program, a computer application.

shenty/-ys (pl.): *Pascentis lentuli* ("slow/methodical grazer"), commonly known as "shenty" is a form of woolly grazing animal, smaller than Earth sheep but analogous to them, native to Centauri and farmed for meat and wool. In the 31st century, the origin of the name "shenty" is unknown.

Shinna Caldones: a Xerxian clan composed of the descendants of Scottish immigrants to Xerxes. The name is a bastardized blend of Gaelic and Latin words (for *Caledonian Clan*) and aligns this faction with the harsh living conditions of the early Picts three thousand years before.

shippy: Peacekeeper slang for Navy personnel.

tualedna oostee: A Polluxan insult with Serbian roots. Literally, *toilet mouth*.

More Westermann?

WESTERMANN REAPPEARS as an important support character in the *ENVOYS* trilogy, commencing with the novel *Third Contact*.

But she also has another story of her own...

The novelette *Shore Leave* is set 12 years after *Exclusion Zone* and just before *ENVOYS*. And it's an extension of her story from *Exclusion Zone*.

Novelette means a short novella (or very long short story). *Shore Leave* is ebook only and it's **completely free** as a thank you when you sign up for email updates from the author. Use the QR code below, or go to https:// subscribepage.io/shoreleave to register for *your* free ebook:

PETER J ALDIN

Afterthoughts and Thank Yous

A note in regard to nuclear weapons and the deadly materials used in their manufacture…

I discovered two clear (and clearly argued) schools of thought about this, both online and among my own friends. *One school of thought* states that the Chinese weapons mentioned in EXCLUSION ZONE simply wouldn't last 800 years or more and be in a useful state for repurposing. *The other* states that yes, the shells and working parts would be long gone, *but the nuclear material* would still be useful for people dumb enough to collect it.

I obviously chose to go with the second set of opinions in my story here.

Originally, Stepka had two kids present, a boy and a younger girl. On the advice of my writing group, I combined them into one person. I'm glad I did: Gerrit is a stronger, sharper, richer character for it. And the story is snappier.

There are, as always, many people whose assistance on this novel I'm grateful for.

The Kickstarter backers who raised funds to make this happen. Love you, folks!

Ian, Davidh, Bb and Noel: for outstanding beta reads and editing runs.

Sheena, Janine and Mark for solid final proofreads.

Ivan for the original Kickstarter version cover art (that was exactly how I pictured Westermann at this age). Alexandre for continuing to brand this series so beautifully.

See *you* in the next book. In the meantime, happy reading!

- Pete Aldin (September 2023)